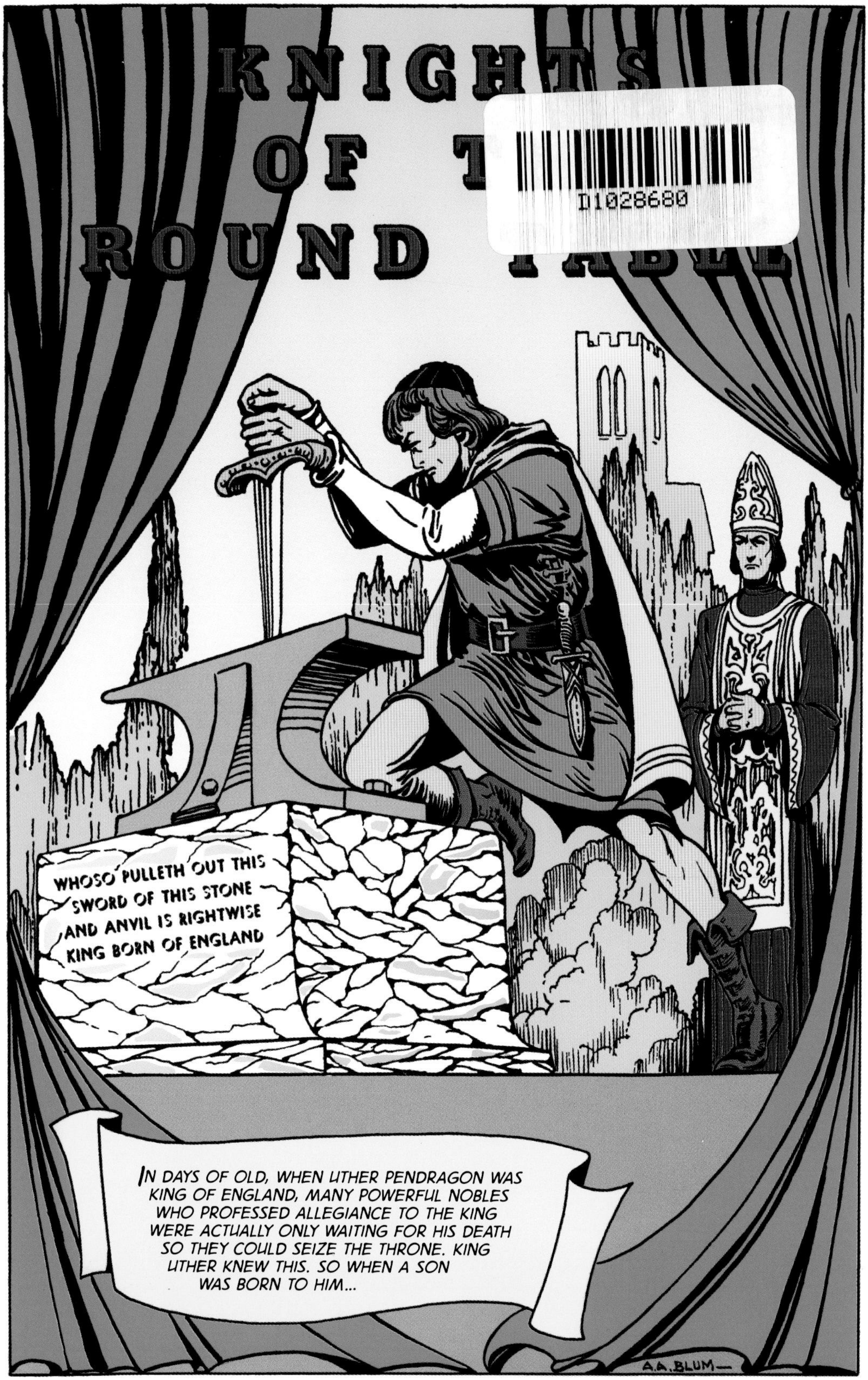

KNIGHTS OF THE ROUND TABLE
WHOSO PULLETH OUT THIS SWORD OF THIS STONE AND ANVIL IS RIGHTWISE KING BORN OF ENGLAND
IN DAYS OF OLD, WHEN UTHER PENDRAGON WAS KING OF ENGLAND, MANY POWERFUL NOBLES WHO PROFESSED ALLEGIANCE TO THE KING WERE ACTUALLY ONLY WAITING FOR HIS DEATH SO THEY COULD SEIZE THE THRONE. KING UTHER KNEW THIS. SO WHEN A SON WAS BORN TO HIM...
A.A. BLUM

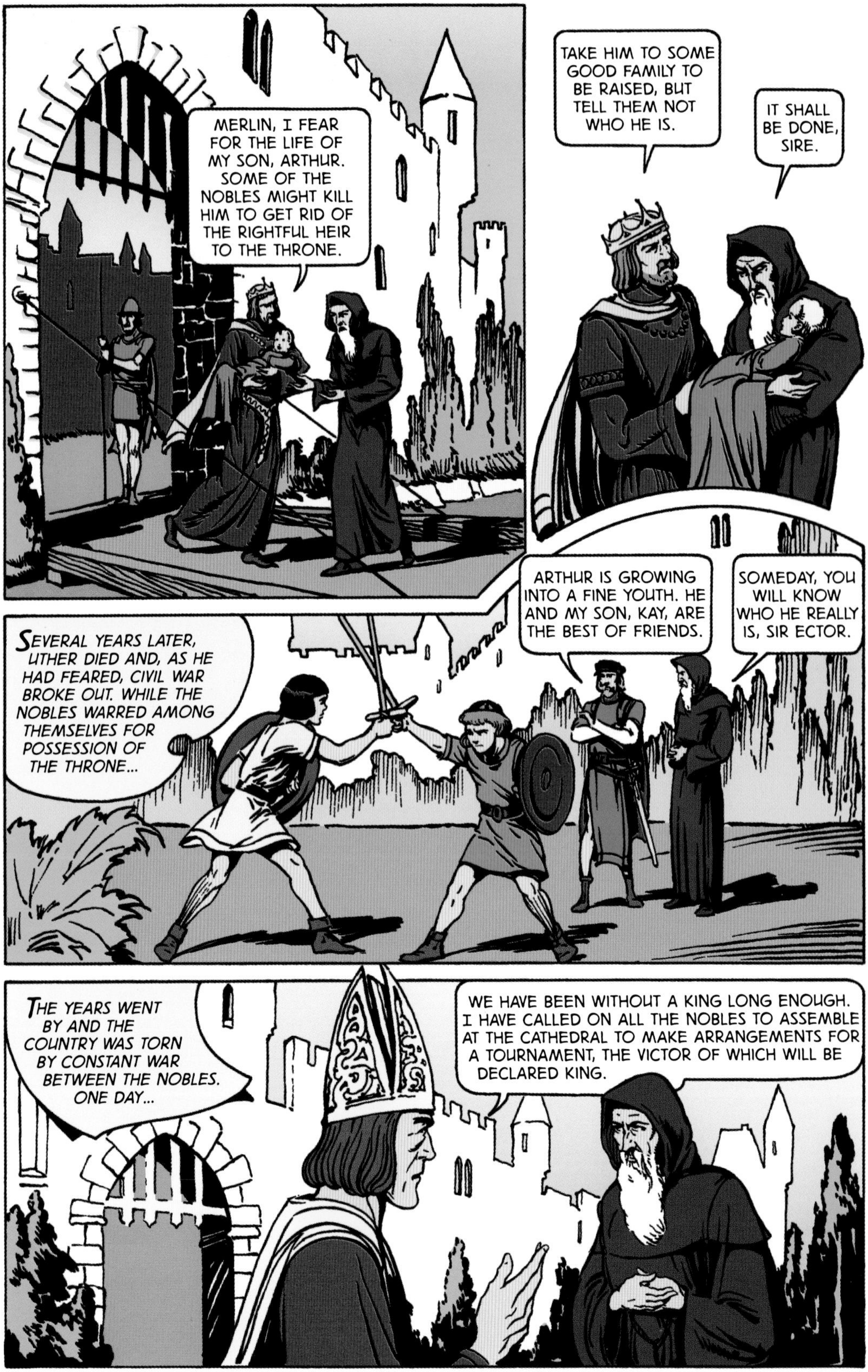
MERLIN, I FEAR FOR THE LIFE OF MY SON, ARTHUR. SOME OF THE NOBLES MIGHT KILL HIM TO GET RID OF THE RIGHTFUL HEIR TO THE THRONE.
TAKE HIM TO SOME GOOD FAMILY TO BE RAISED, BUT TELL THEM NOT WHO HE IS.
IT SHALL BE DONE, SIRE.
SEVERAL YEARS LATER, UTHER DIED AND, AS HE HAD FEARED, CIVIL WAR BROKE OUT. WHILE THE NOBLES WARRED AMONG THEMSELVES FOR POSSESSION OF THE THRONE...
ARTHUR IS GROWING INTO A FINE YOUTH. HE AND MY SON, KAY, ARE THE BEST OF FRIENDS.
SOMEDAY, YOU WILL KNOW WHO HE REALLY IS, SIR ECTOR.
THE YEARS WENT BY AND THE COUNTRY WAS TORN BY CONSTANT WAR BETWEEN THE NOBLES. ONE DAY...
WE HAVE BEEN WITHOUT A KING LONG ENOUGH. I HAVE CALLED ON ALL THE NOBLES TO ASSEMBLE AT THE CATHEDRAL TO MAKE ARRANGEMENTS FOR A TOURNAMENT, THE VICTOR OF WHICH WILL BE DECLARED KING.

AS THE NOBLES GATHERED AT THE CATHEDRAL, THEY SAW IN THE CHURCHYARD...

WHOSO PULLETH OUT THIS SWORD OF THIS STONE AND ANVIL IS RIGHTWISE KING BORN OF ENGLAND

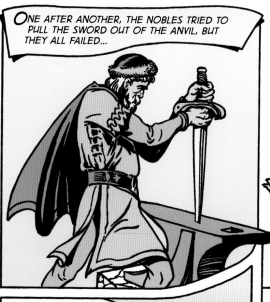

ONE AFTER ANOTHER, THE NOBLES TRIED TO PULL THE SWORD OUT OF THE ANVIL, BUT THEY ALL FAILED...

EVIDENTLY, THE RIGHTFUL KING HAS NOT YET ARRIVED. PERHAPS HE WILL BE HERE TOMORROW. WE WILL HOLD THE TOURNAMENT AS PLANNED.

ARTHUR RODE HOME, BUT COULD NOT FIND KAY'S SWORD. ON THE WAY BACK TO THE FIELD, HE PASSED THE CHURCHYARD...

I'LL TAKE THIS ONE FOR MY BROTHER.

THE NEXT DAY...

THE TOURNAMENT FIELD IS JUST AHEAD, KAY.

I LEFT MY SWORD AT HOME! ARTHUR, WILL YOU SEE IF YOU CAN GET ONE FOR ME SO I CAN ENTER THE TOURNAMENT?

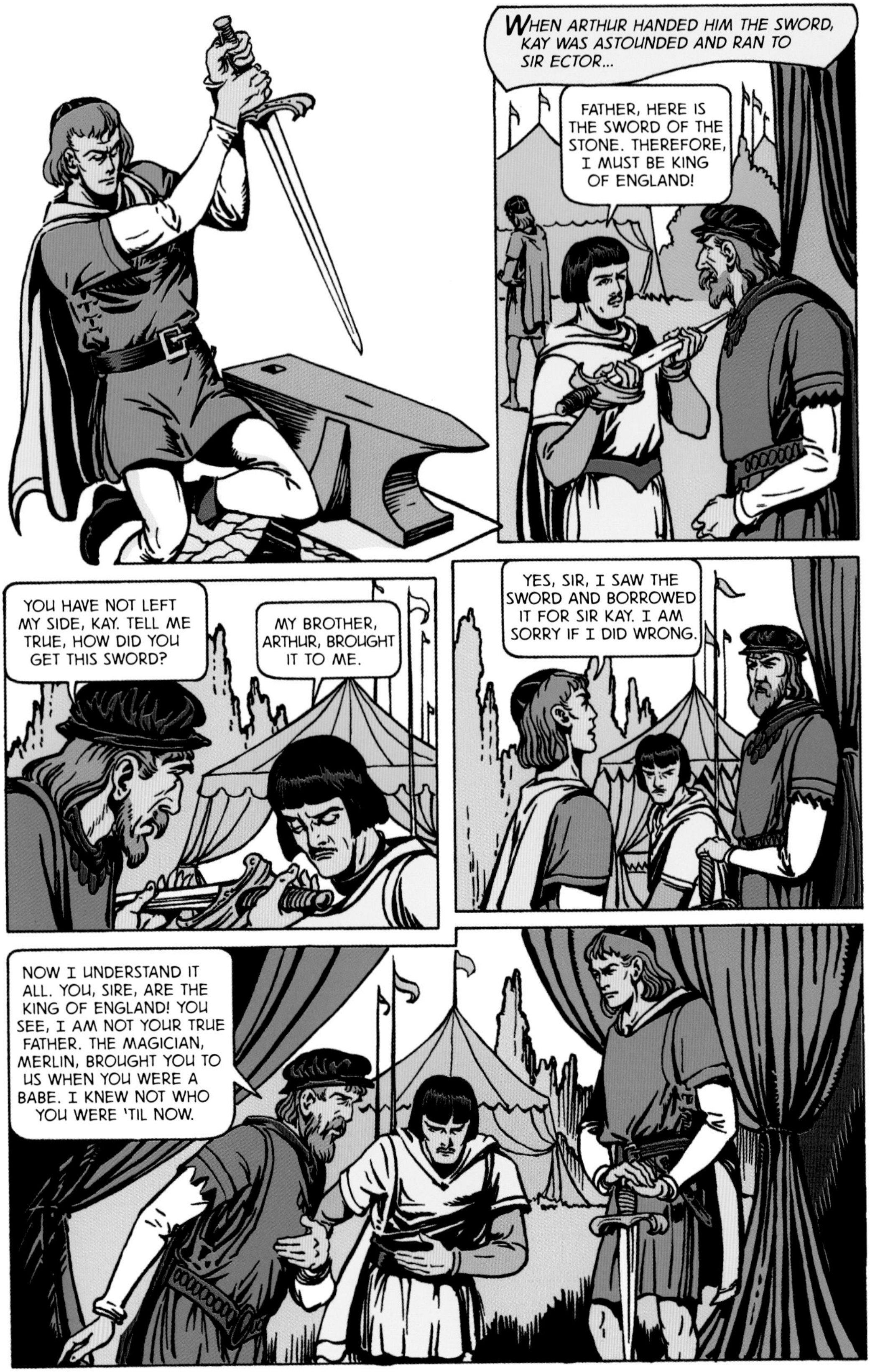
WHEN ARTHUR HANDED HIM THE SWORD, KAY WAS ASTOUNDED AND RAN TO SIR ECTOR...
FATHER, HERE IS THE SWORD OF THE STONE. THEREFORE, I MUST BE KING OF ENGLAND!
YOU HAVE NOT LEFT MY SIDE, KAY. TELL ME TRUE, HOW DID YOU GET THIS SWORD?
MY BROTHER, ARTHUR, BROUGHT IT TO ME.
YES, SIR, I SAW THE SWORD AND BORROWED IT FOR SIR KAY. I AM SORRY IF I DID WRONG.
NOW I UNDERSTAND IT ALL. YOU, SIRE, ARE THE KING OF ENGLAND! YOU SEE, I AM NOT YOUR TRUE FATHER. THE MAGICIAN, MERLIN, BROUGHT YOU TO US WHEN YOU WERE A BABE. I KNEW NOT WHO YOU WERE 'TIL NOW.

LATER...

REPLACE THE SWORD IN THE ANVIL, MY LORD. THEN THE OTHER NOBLES WILL TRY AGAIN.

WHOSO PULLETH OUT THIS SWORD OF THIS STONE AND ANVIL IS RIGHTWISE KING BORN OF ENGLAND

AGAIN THE NOBLES TRIED AND AGAIN THEY FAILED...

THEN ARTHUR WAS PUT TO THE TEST...

HE PULLED IT OUT EASILY!

HE IS THE TRUE KING OF ENGLAND! LONG LIVE THE KING! LONG LIVE KING ARTHUR!

WHOSO PULLETH OUT THIS SWORD OF THIS STONE AND ANVIL IS RIGHTWISE KING BORN OF ENGLAND

SHORTLY AFTER ARTHUR'S CORONATION...

SIRE, A SHORT DISTANCE FROM HERE, WE SHALL GET YOU A SWORD WORTHY OF A GREAT KING.

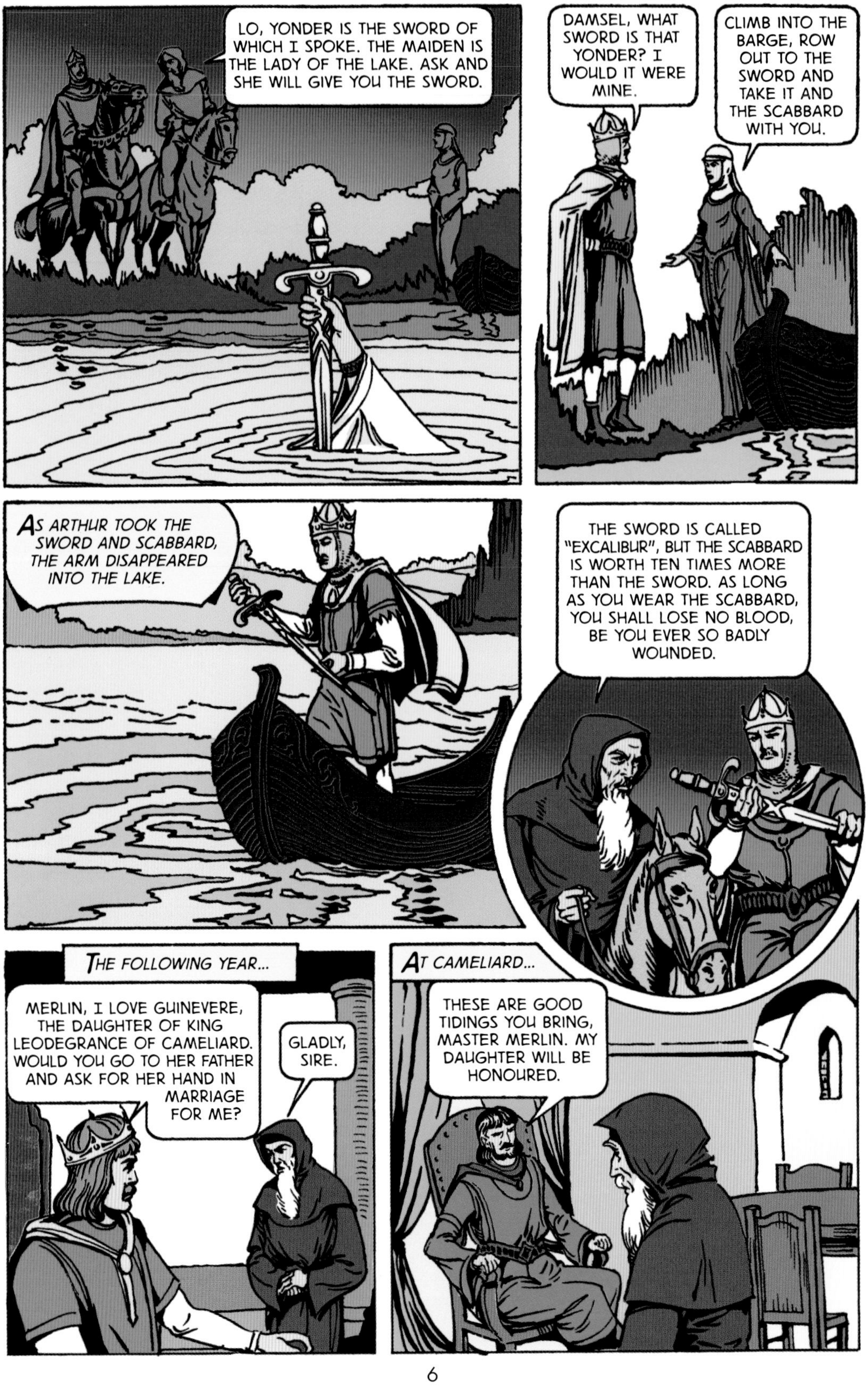
LO, YONDER IS THE SWORD OF WHICH I SPOKE. THE MAIDEN IS THE LADY OF THE LAKE. ASK AND SHE WILL GIVE YOU THE SWORD.
DAMSEL, WHAT SWORD IS THAT YONDER? I WOULD IT WERE MINE.
CLIMB INTO THE BARGE, ROW OUT TO THE SWORD AND TAKE IT AND THE SCABBARD WITH YOU.
AS ARTHUR TOOK THE SWORD AND SCABBARD, THE ARM DISAPPEARED INTO THE LAKE.
THE SWORD IS CALLED "EXCALIBUR", BUT THE SCABBARD IS WORTH TEN TIMES MORE THAN THE SWORD. AS LONG AS YOU WEAR THE SCABBARD, YOU SHALL LOSE NO BLOOD, BE YOU EVER SO BADLY WOUNDED.
THE FOLLOWING YEAR...
MERLIN, I LOVE GUINEVERE, THE DAUGHTER OF KING LEODEGRANCE OF CAMELIARD. WOULD YOU GO TO HER FATHER AND ASK FOR HER HAND IN MARRIAGE FOR ME?
GLADLY, SIRE.
AT CAMELIARD...
THESE ARE GOOD TIDINGS YOU BRING, MASTER MERLIN. MY DAUGHTER WILL BE HONOURED.

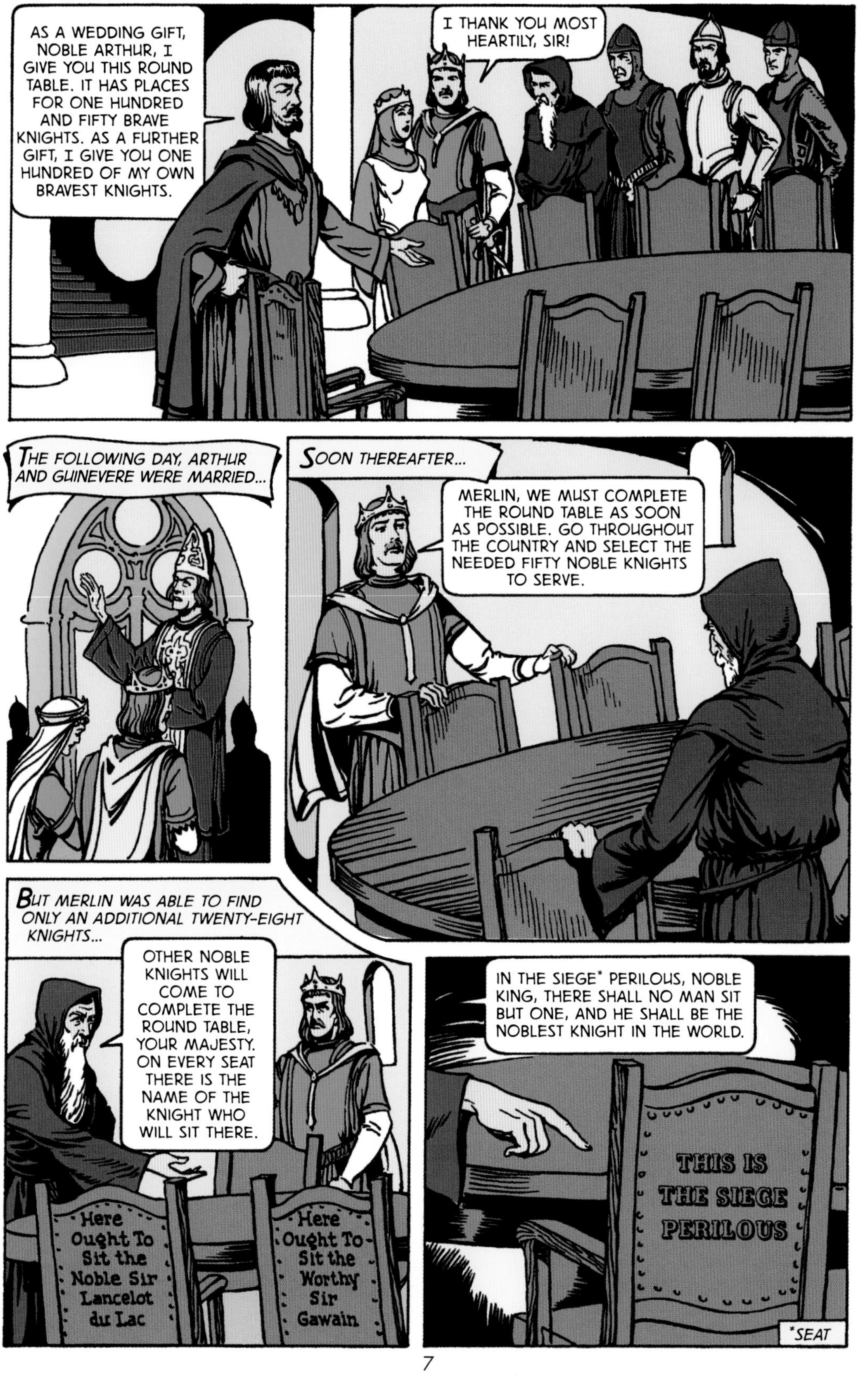
AS A WEDDING GIFT, NOBLE ARTHUR, I GIVE YOU THIS ROUND TABLE. IT HAS PLACES FOR ONE HUNDRED AND FIFTY BRAVE KNIGHTS. AS A FURTHER GIFT, I GIVE YOU ONE HUNDRED OF MY OWN BRAVEST KNIGHTS.
I THANK YOU MOST HEARTILY, SIR!
THE FOLLOWING DAY, ARTHUR AND GUINEVERE WERE MARRIED...
SOON THEREAFTER...
MERLIN, WE MUST COMPLETE THE ROUND TABLE AS SOON AS POSSIBLE. GO THROUGHOUT THE COUNTRY AND SELECT THE NEEDED FIFTY NOBLE KNIGHTS TO SERVE.
BUT MERLIN WAS ABLE TO FIND ONLY AN ADDITIONAL TWENTY-EIGHT KNIGHTS...
OTHER NOBLE KNIGHTS WILL COME TO COMPLETE THE ROUND TABLE, YOUR MAJESTY. ON EVERY SEAT THERE IS THE NAME OF THE KNIGHT WHO WILL SIT THERE.
Here Ought To Sit the Noble Sir Lancelot du Lac
Here Ought To Sit the Worthy Sir Gawain
IN THE SIEGE* PERILOUS, NOBLE KING, THERE SHALL NO MAN SIT BUT ONE, AND HE SHALL BE THE NOBLEST KNIGHT IN THE WORLD.
THIS IS THE SIEGE PERILOUS
*SEAT

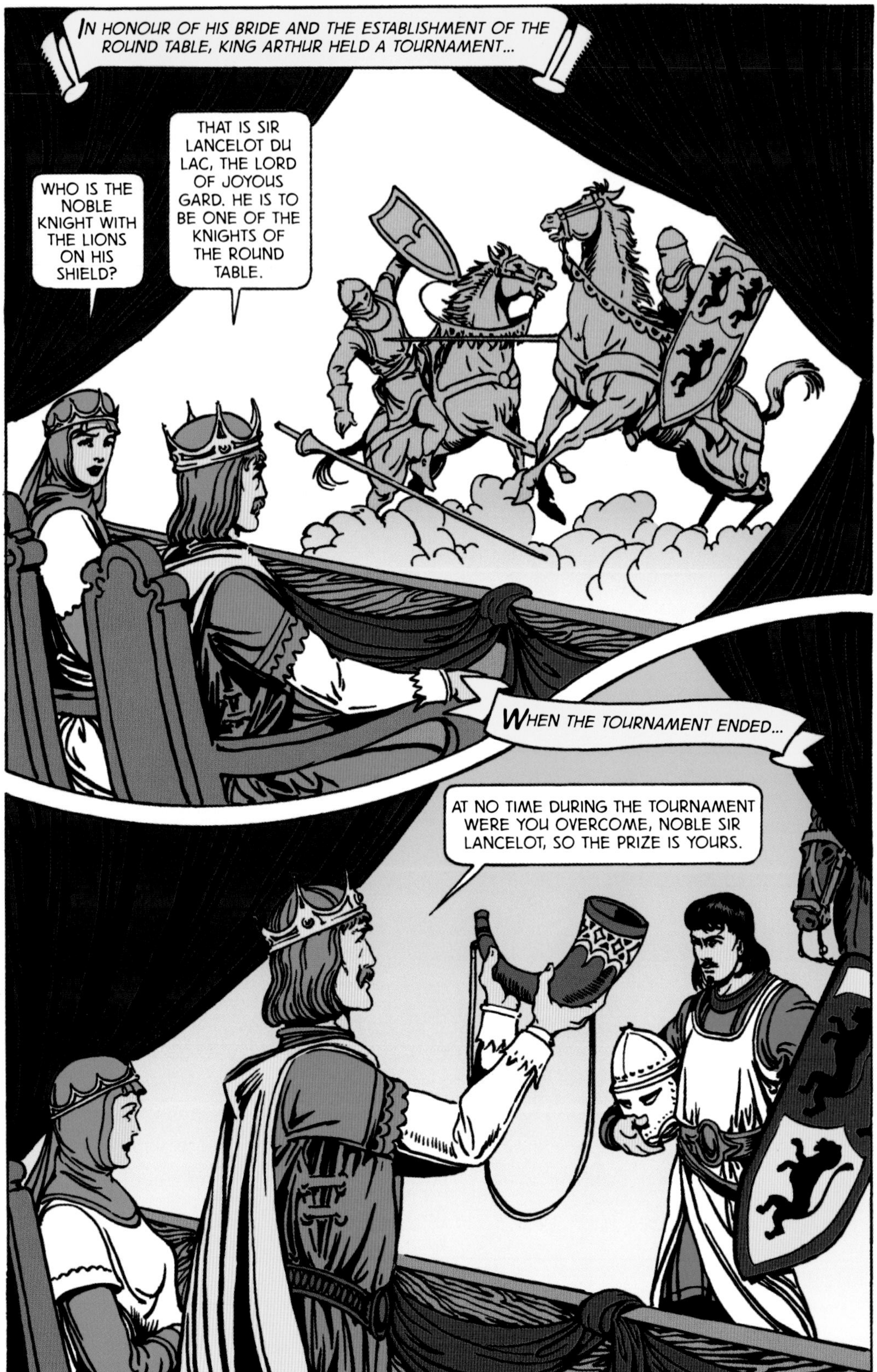
IN HONOUR OF HIS BRIDE AND THE ESTABLISHMENT OF THE ROUND TABLE, KING ARTHUR HELD A TOURNAMENT...
WHO IS THE NOBLE KNIGHT WITH THE LIONS ON HIS SHIELD?
THAT IS SIR LANCELOT DU LAC, THE LORD OF JOYOUS GARD. HE IS TO BE ONE OF THE KNIGHTS OF THE ROUND TABLE.
WHEN THE TOURNAMENT ENDED...
AT NO TIME DURING THE TOURNAMENT WERE YOU OVERCOME, NOBLE SIR LANCELOT, SO THE PRIZE IS YOURS.

THE FAME OF THE ROUND TABLE SPREAD THROUGH ENGLAND. MANY PEOPLE CAME ASKING ARTHUR TO SEND THE KNIGHTS TO HELP REDRESS WRONGS DONE THEM...

WHAT DO YOU WANT, MY SON? ASK AND YOU SHALL HAVE YOUR ASKING.

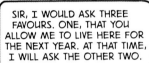

SIR, I WOULD ASK THREE FAVOURS. ONE, THAT YOU ALLOW ME TO LIVE HERE FOR THE NEXT YEAR. AT THAT TIME, I WILL ASK THE OTHER TWO.

YOU SHALL HAVE YOUR WISH, BUT WHAT IS YOUR NAME?

SIR, THAT I CANNOT TELL YOU NOW.

VERY WELL. SIR KAY, WILL YOU SEE THAT THIS NOBLE YOUTH IS TAKEN CARE OF?

NOBLE, HMPF. I DOUBT NOT THAT HE IS A THIEF OR WORSE, SINCE HE REFUSES TO TELL HIS NAME. I SHALL CALL HIM BEAUMAINS.*

*FAIR HANDS

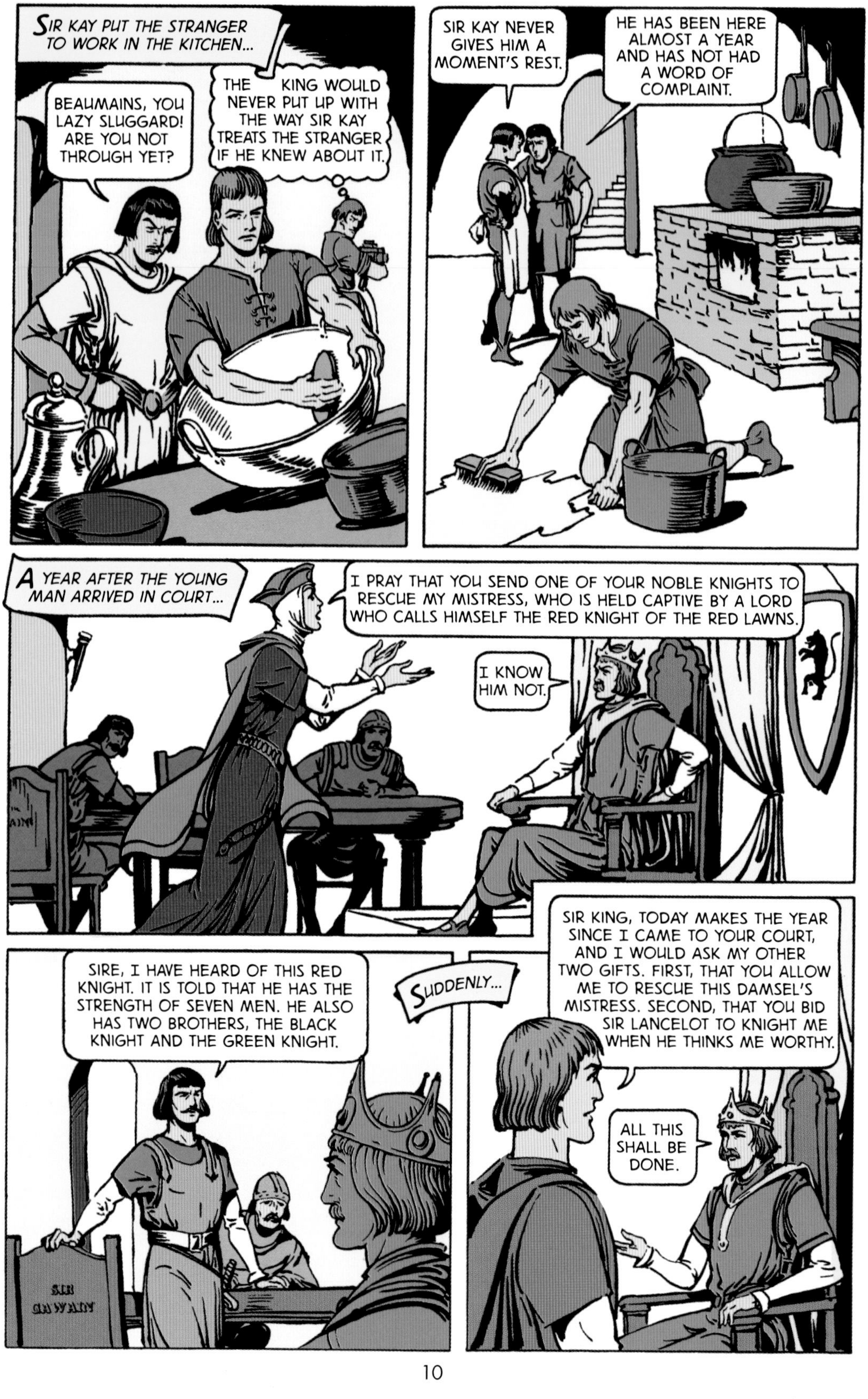
SIR KAY PUT THE STRANGER TO WORK IN THE KITCHEN...
BEAUMAINS, YOU LAZY SLUGGARD! ARE YOU NOT THROUGH YET?
THE KING WOULD NEVER PUT UP WITH THE WAY SIR KAY TREATS THE STRANGER IF HE KNEW ABOUT IT.
SIR KAY NEVER GIVES HIM A MOMENT'S REST.
HE HAS BEEN HERE ALMOST A YEAR AND HAS NOT HAD A WORD OF COMPLAINT.
A YEAR AFTER THE YOUNG MAN ARRIVED IN COURT...
I PRAY THAT YOU SEND ONE OF YOUR NOBLE KNIGHTS TO RESCUE MY MISTRESS, WHO IS HELD CAPTIVE BY A LORD WHO CALLS HIMSELF THE RED KNIGHT OF THE RED LAWNS.
I KNOW HIM NOT.
SIRE, I HAVE HEARD OF THIS RED KNIGHT. IT IS TOLD THAT HE HAS THE STRENGTH OF SEVEN MEN. HE ALSO HAS TWO BROTHERS, THE BLACK KNIGHT AND THE GREEN KNIGHT.
SIR GAWAIN
SUDDENLY...
SIR KING, TODAY MAKES THE YEAR SINCE I CAME TO YOUR COURT, AND I WOULD ASK MY OTHER TWO GIFTS. FIRST, THAT YOU ALLOW ME TO RESCUE THIS DAMSEL'S MISTRESS. SECOND, THAT YOU BID SIR LANCELOT TO KNIGHT ME WHEN HE THINKS ME WORTHY.
ALL THIS SHALL BE DONE.

SHALL I HAVE NONE TO RESCUE MY MISTRESS BUT ONE WHO IS YOUR KITCHEN PAGE?

NONE.

SUDDENLY A DWARF APPEARED WITH A HORSE AND ARMOUR FOR BEAUMAINS...

I HAVE RARELY SEEN SUCH GOODLY ARMOUR.

AND SO FINE A WARHORSE.

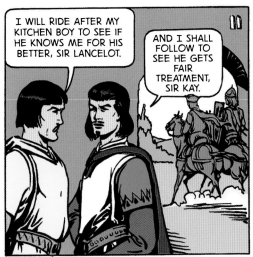

I WILL RIDE AFTER MY KITCHEN BOY TO SEE IF HE KNOWS ME FOR HIS BETTER, SIR LANCELOT.

AND I SHALL FOLLOW TO SEE HE GETS FAIR TREATMENT, SIR KAY.

WHAT DO YOU DO HERE? YOU SMELL OF KITCHEN GREASE. GO BACK TO YOUR POTS AND PANS!

THEN...

BEAUMAINS, DO YOU KNOW YOUR MASTER? DEFEND YOURSELF, KITCHEN PAGE!

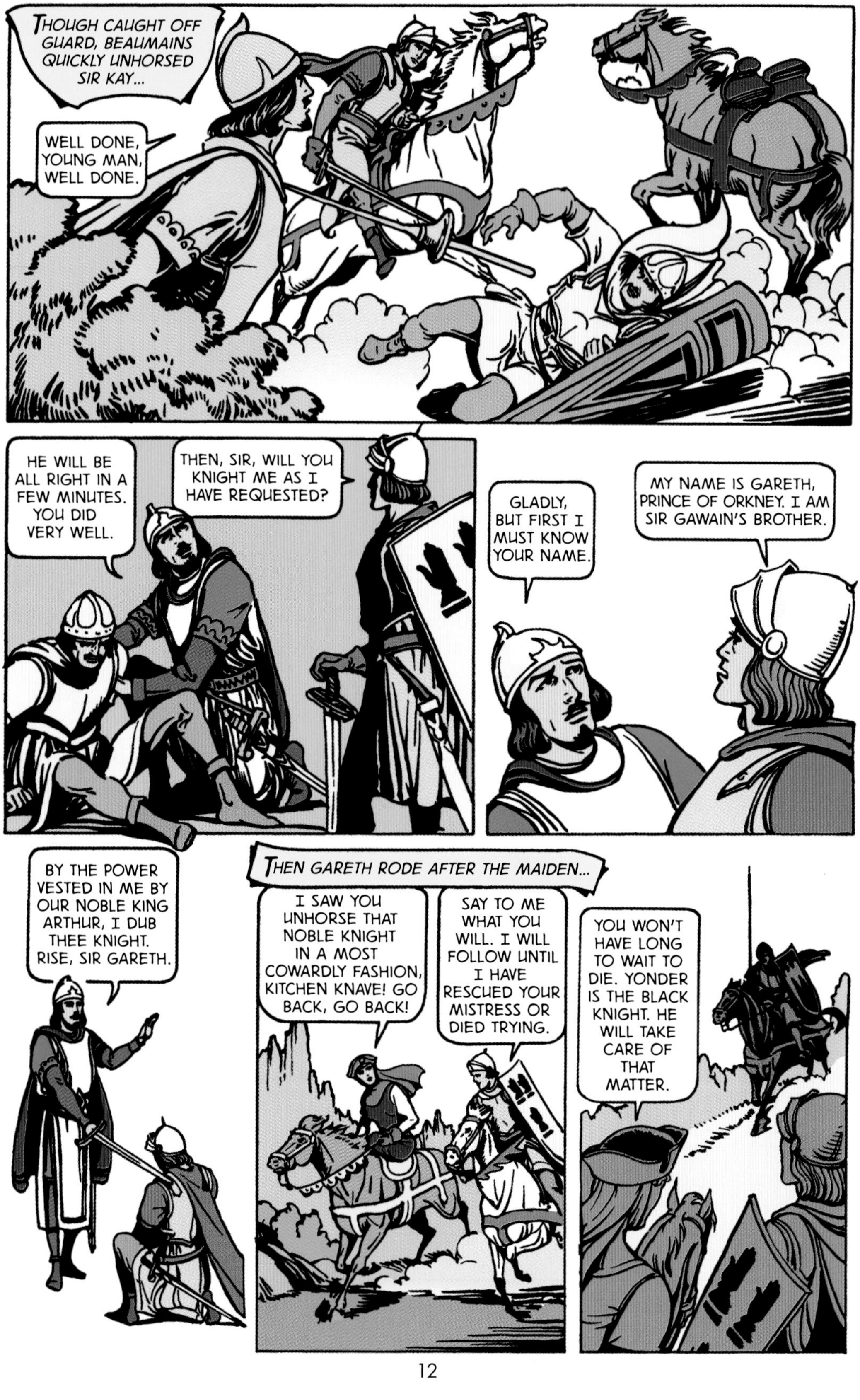
THOUGH CAUGHT OFF GUARD, BEAUMAINS QUICKLY UNHORSED SIR KAY...
WELL DONE, YOUNG MAN, WELL DONE.
HE WILL BE ALL RIGHT IN A FEW MINUTES. YOU DID VERY WELL.
THEN, SIR, WILL YOU KNIGHT ME AS I HAVE REQUESTED?
GLADLY, BUT FIRST I MUST KNOW YOUR NAME.
MY NAME IS GARETH, PRINCE OF ORKNEY. I AM SIR GAWAIN'S BROTHER.
BY THE POWER VESTED IN ME BY OUR NOBLE KING ARTHUR, I DUB THEE KNIGHT. RISE, SIR GARETH.
THEN GARETH RODE AFTER THE MAIDEN...
I SAW YOU UNHORSE THAT NOBLE KNIGHT IN A MOST COWARDLY FASHION, KITCHEN KNAVE! GO BACK, GO BACK!
SAY TO ME WHAT YOU WILL. I WILL FOLLOW UNTIL I HAVE RESCUED YOUR MISTRESS OR DIED TRYING.
YOU WON'T HAVE LONG TO WAIT TO DIE. YONDER IS THE BLACK KNIGHT. HE WILL TAKE CARE OF THAT MATTER.

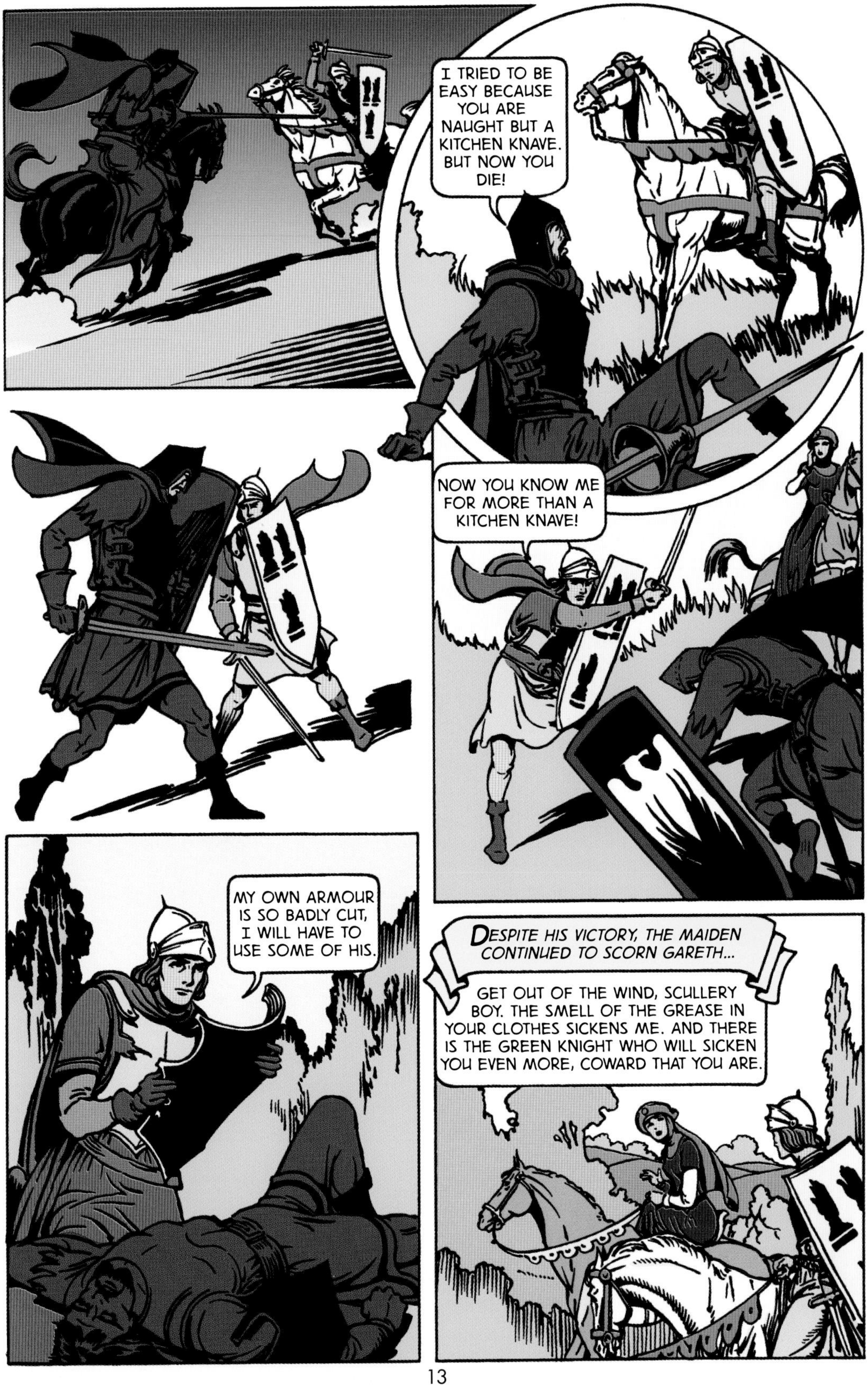
I TRIED TO BE EASY BECAUSE YOU ARE NAUGHT BUT A KITCHEN KNAVE. BUT NOW YOU DIE!
NOW YOU KNOW ME FOR MORE THAN A KITCHEN KNAVE!
MY OWN ARMOUR IS SO BADLY CUT, I WILL HAVE TO USE SOME OF HIS.
DESPITE HIS VICTORY, THE MAIDEN CONTINUED TO SCORN GARETH...
GET OUT OF THE WIND, SCULLERY BOY. THE SMELL OF THE GREASE IN YOUR CLOTHES SICKENS ME. AND THERE IS THE GREEN KNIGHT WHO WILL SICKEN YOU EVEN MORE, COWARD THAT YOU ARE.

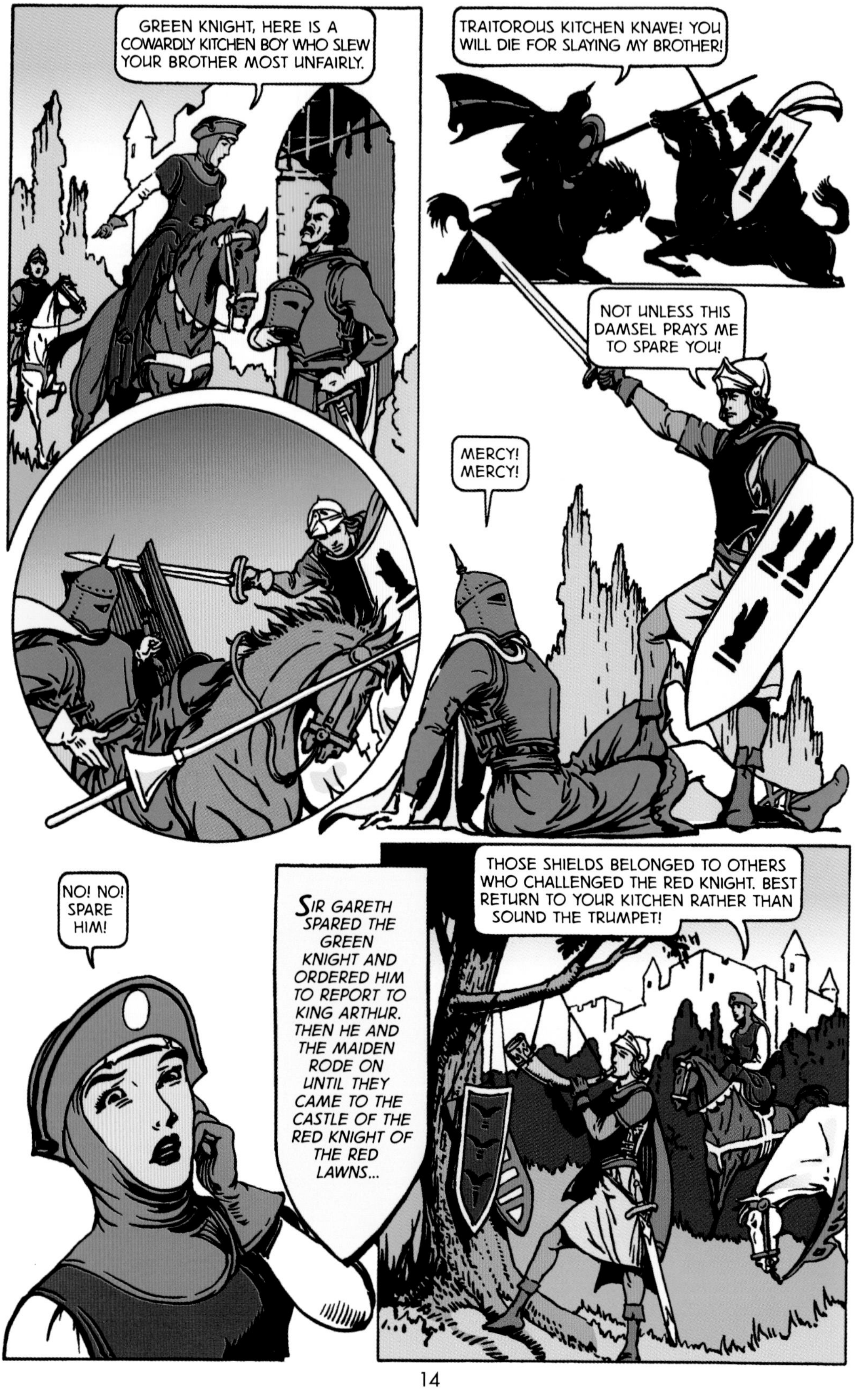
GREEN KNIGHT, HERE IS A COWARDLY KITCHEN BOY WHO SLEW YOUR BROTHER MOST UNFAIRLY.
TRAITOROUS KITCHEN KNAVE! YOU WILL DIE FOR SLAYING MY BROTHER!
NOT UNLESS THIS DAMSEL PRAYS ME TO SPARE YOU!
MERCY! MERCY!
NO! NO! SPARE HIM!
SIR GARETH SPARED THE GREEN KNIGHT AND ORDERED HIM TO REPORT TO KING ARTHUR. THEN HE AND THE MAIDEN RODE ON UNTIL THEY CAME TO THE CASTLE OF THE RED KNIGHT OF THE RED LAWNS...
THOSE SHIELDS BELONGED TO OTHERS WHO CHALLENGED THE RED KNIGHT. BEST RETURN TO YOUR KITCHEN RATHER THAN SOUND THE TRUMPET!

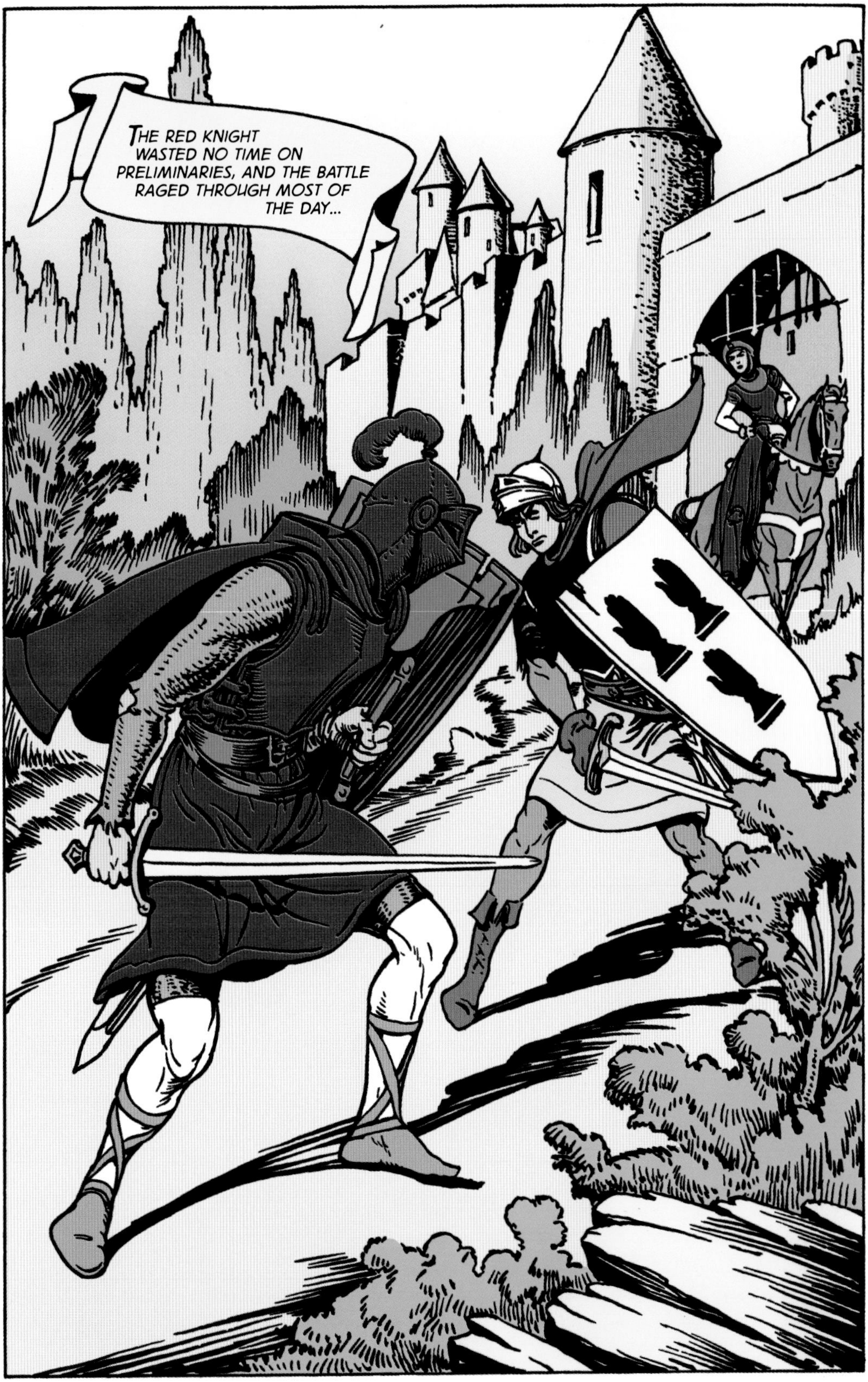
THE RED KNIGHT WASTED NO TIME ON PRELIMINARIES, AND THE BATTLE RAGED THROUGH MOST OF THE DAY...

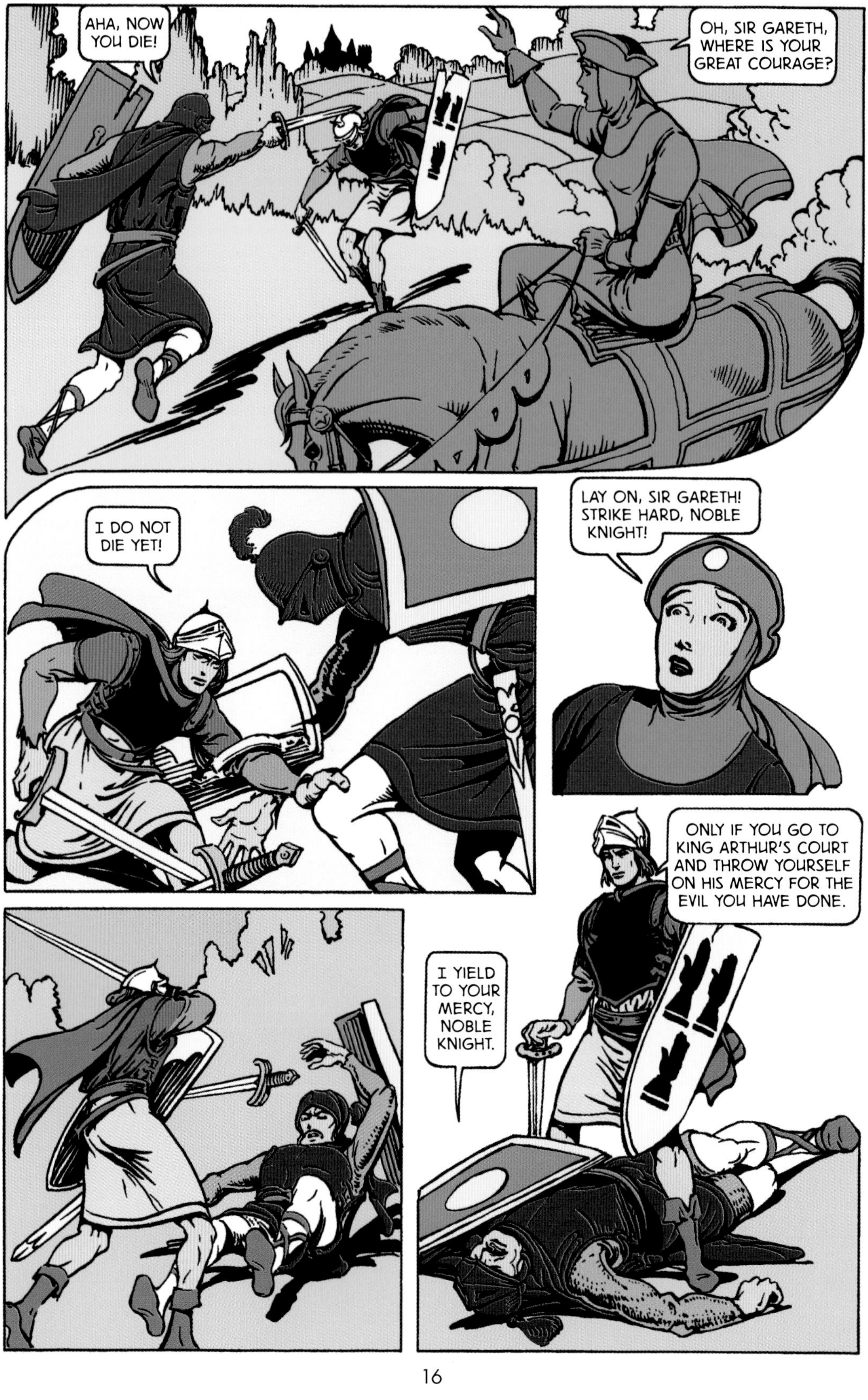
AHA, NOW YOU DIE!
OH, SIR GARETH, WHERE IS YOUR GREAT COURAGE?
I DO NOT DIE YET!
LAY ON, SIR GARETH! STRIKE HARD, NOBLE KNIGHT!
I YIELD TO YOUR MERCY, NOBLE KNIGHT.
ONLY IF YOU GO TO KING ARTHUR'S COURT AND THROW YOURSELF ON HIS MERCY FOR THE EVIL YOU HAVE DONE.

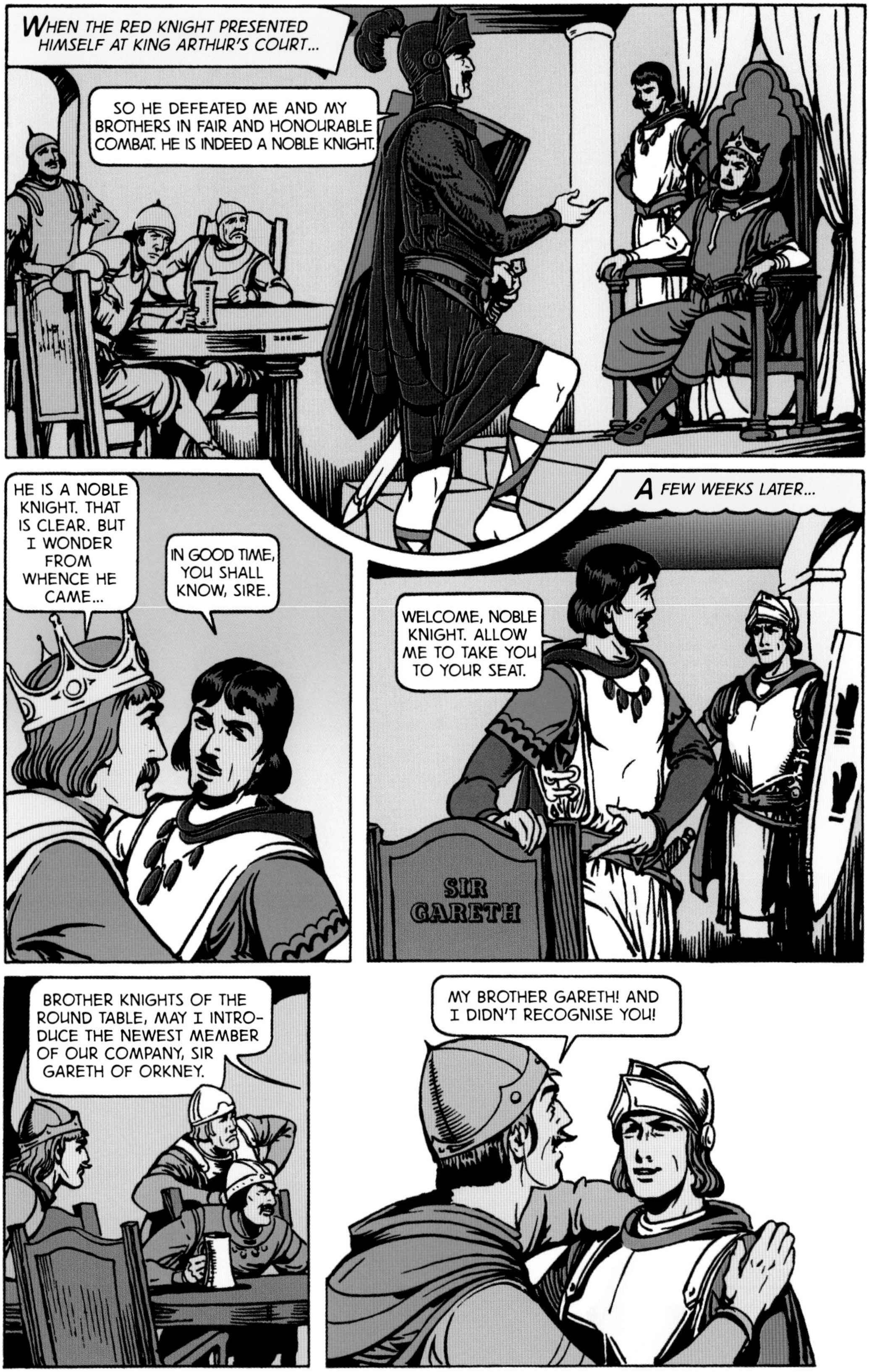
WHEN THE RED KNIGHT PRESENTED HIMSELF AT KING ARTHUR'S COURT...
SO HE DEFEATED ME AND MY BROTHERS IN FAIR AND HONOURABLE COMBAT. HE IS INDEED A NOBLE KNIGHT.
HE IS A NOBLE KNIGHT. THAT IS CLEAR. BUT I WONDER FROM WHENCE HE CAME...
IN GOOD TIME, YOU SHALL KNOW, SIRE.
A FEW WEEKS LATER...
WELCOME, NOBLE KNIGHT. ALLOW ME TO TAKE YOU TO YOUR SEAT.
SIR GARETH
BROTHER KNIGHTS OF THE ROUND TABLE, MAY I INTRODUCE THE NEWEST MEMBER OF OUR COMPANY, SIR GARETH OF ORKNEY.
MY BROTHER GARETH! AND I DIDN'T RECOGNISE YOU!

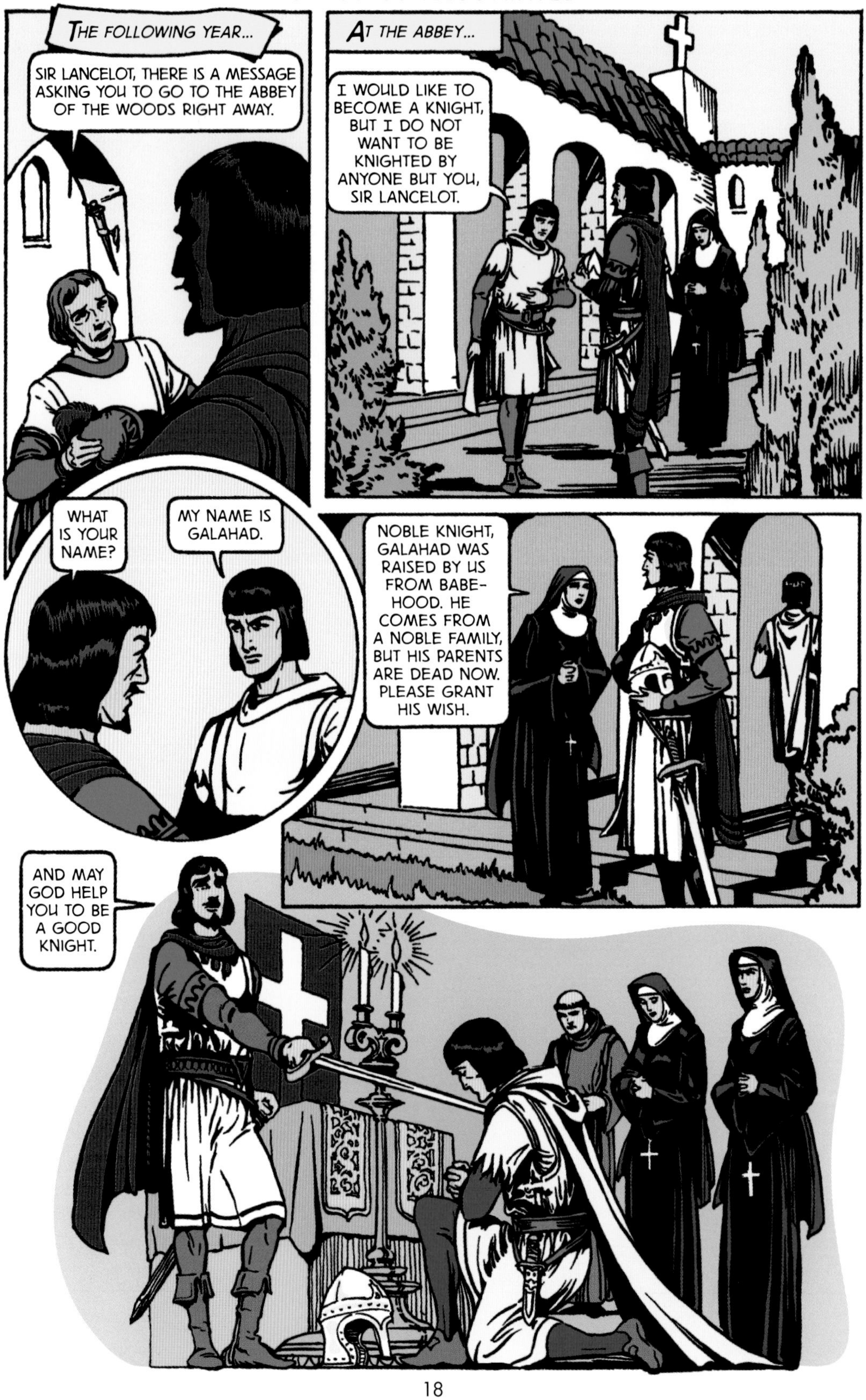
THE FOLLOWING YEAR...
SIR LANCELOT, THERE IS A MESSAGE ASKING YOU TO GO TO THE ABBEY OF THE WOODS RIGHT AWAY.
AT THE ABBEY...
I WOULD LIKE TO BECOME A KNIGHT, BUT I DO NOT WANT TO BE KNIGHTED BY ANYONE BUT YOU, SIR LANCELOT.
WHAT IS YOUR NAME?
MY NAME IS GALAHAD.
NOBLE KNIGHT, GALAHAD WAS RAISED BY US FROM BABE-HOOD. HE COMES FROM A NOBLE FAMILY, BUT HIS PARENTS ARE DEAD NOW. PLEASE GRANT HIS WISH.
AND MAY GOD HELP YOU TO BE A GOOD KNIGHT.

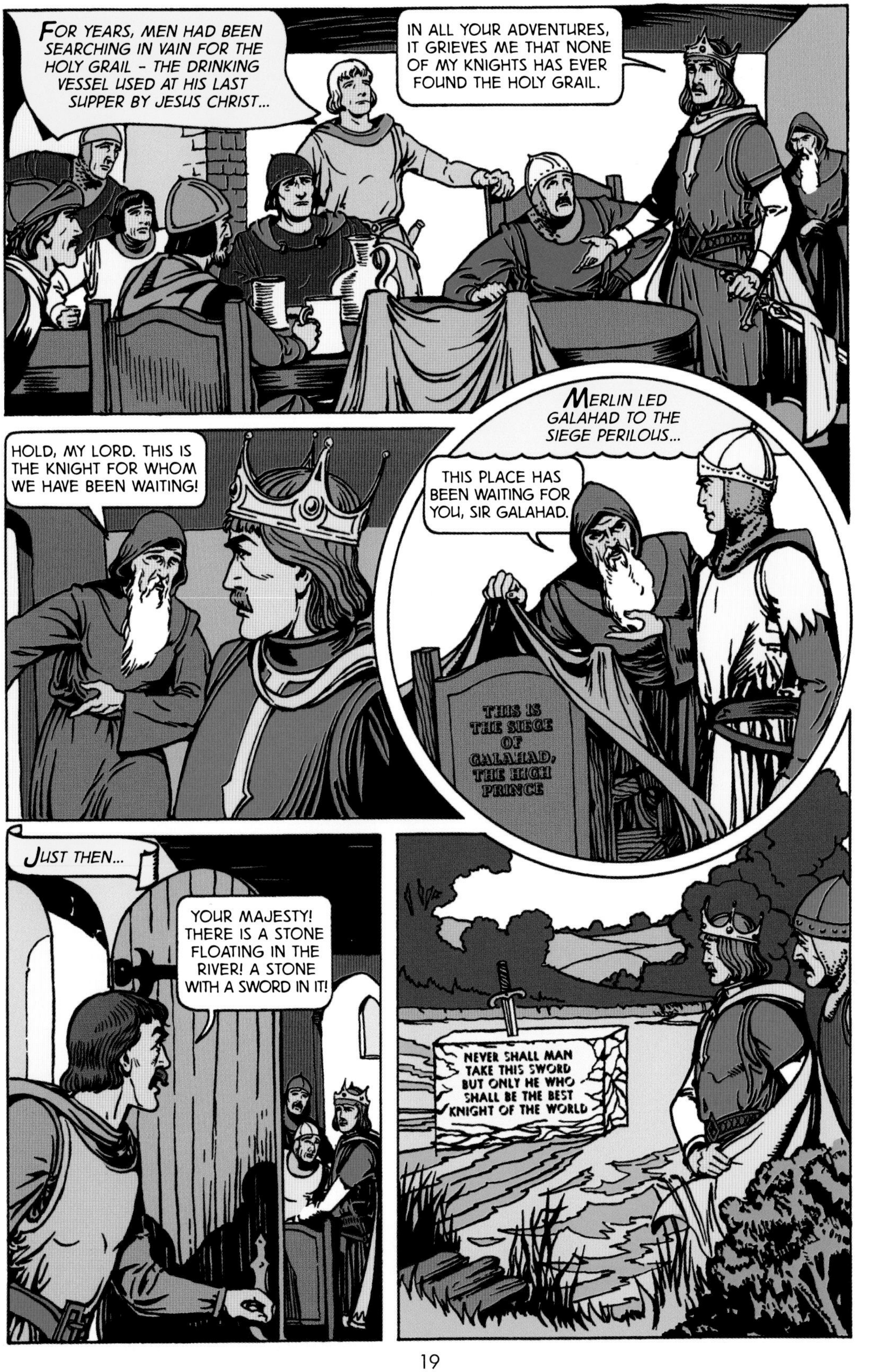
FOR YEARS, MEN HAD BEEN SEARCHING IN VAIN FOR THE HOLY GRAIL - THE DRINKING VESSEL USED AT HIS LAST SUPPER BY JESUS CHRIST...
IN ALL YOUR ADVENTURES, IT GRIEVES ME THAT NONE OF MY KNIGHTS HAS EVER FOUND THE HOLY GRAIL.
HOLD, MY LORD. THIS IS THE KNIGHT FOR WHOM WE HAVE BEEN WAITING!
MERLIN LED GALAHAD TO THE SIEGE PERILOUS...
THIS PLACE HAS BEEN WAITING FOR YOU, SIR GALAHAD.
THIS IS THE SIEGE OF GALAHAD, THE HIGH PRINCE
JUST THEN...
YOUR MAJESTY! THERE IS A STONE FLOATING IN THE RIVER! A STONE WITH A SWORD IN IT!
NEVER SHALL MAN TAKE THIS SWORD BUT ONLY HE WHO SHALL BE THE BEST KNIGHT OF THE WORLD

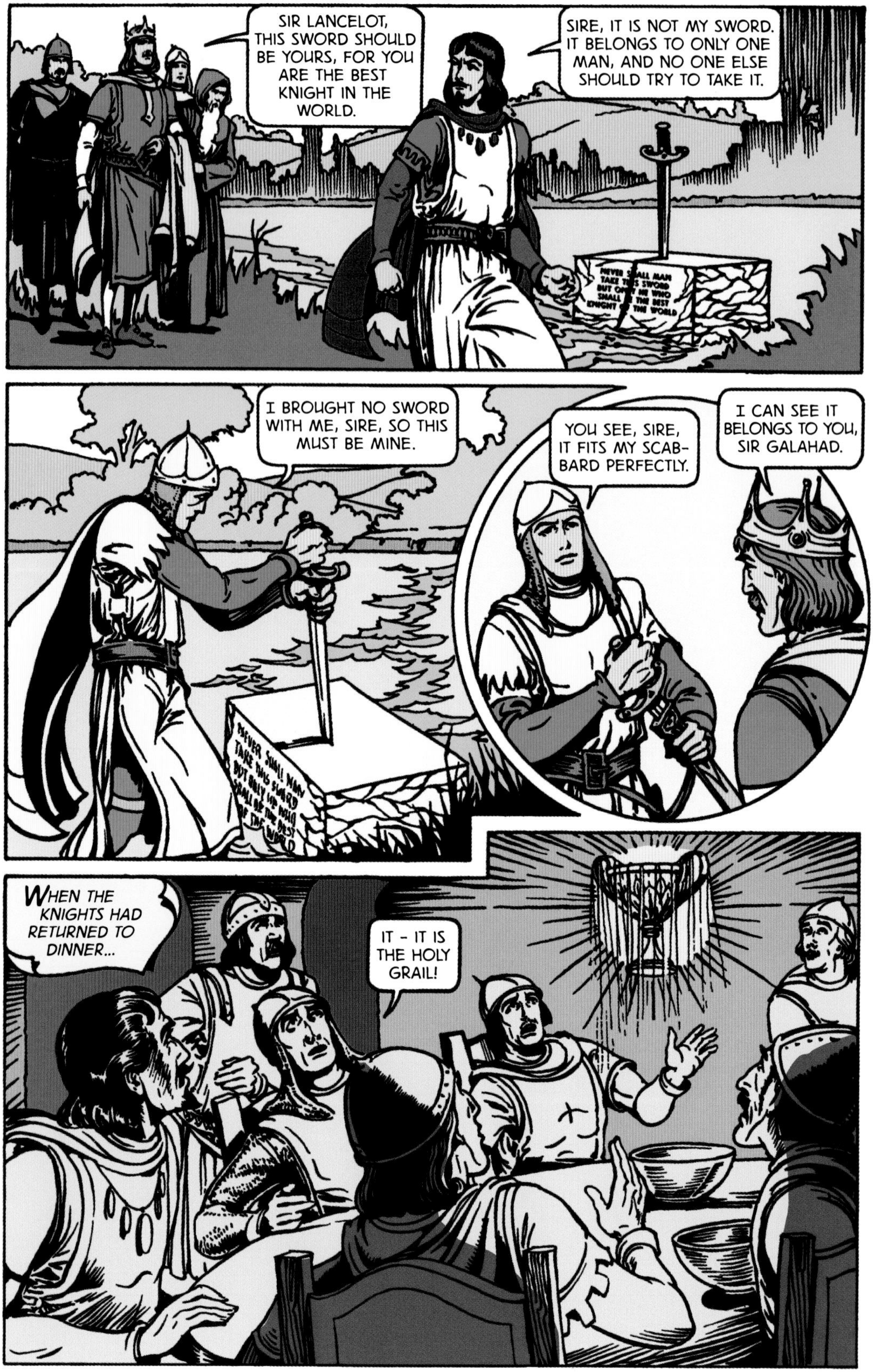
SIR LANCELOT, THIS SWORD SHOULD BE YOURS, FOR YOU ARE THE BEST KNIGHT IN THE WORLD.
SIRE, IT IS NOT MY SWORD. IT BELONGS TO ONLY ONE MAN, AND NO ONE ELSE SHOULD TRY TO TAKE IT.
I BROUGHT NO SWORD WITH ME, SIRE, SO THIS MUST BE MINE.
YOU SEE, SIRE, IT FITS MY SCAB-BARD PERFECTLY.
I CAN SEE IT BELONGS TO YOU, SIR GALAHAD.
WHEN THE KNIGHTS HAD RETURNED TO DINNER...
IT - IT IS THE HOLY GRAIL!

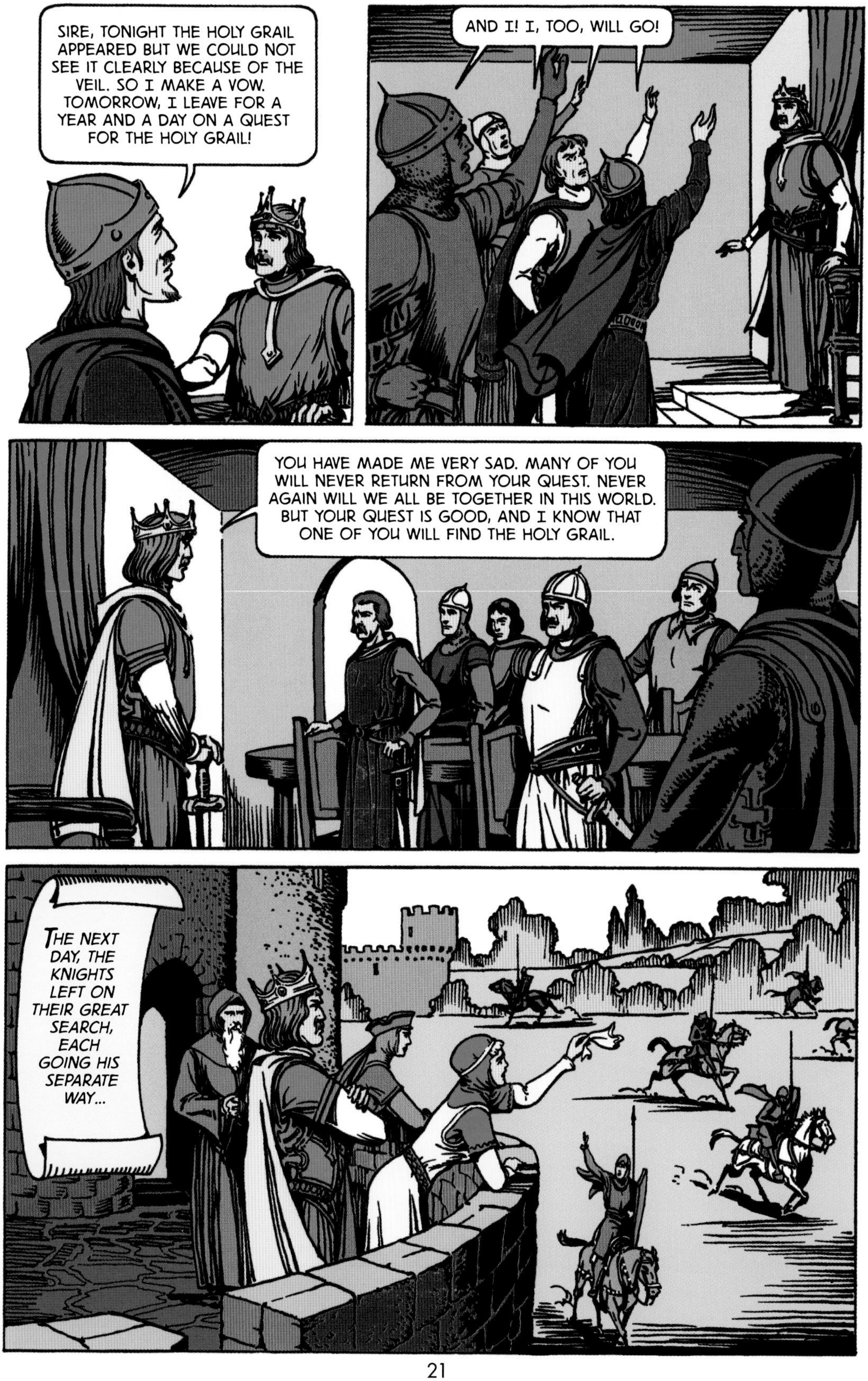
SIRE, TONIGHT THE HOLY GRAIL APPEARED BUT WE COULD NOT SEE IT CLEARLY BECAUSE OF THE VEIL. SO I MAKE A VOW. TOMORROW, I LEAVE FOR A YEAR AND A DAY ON A QUEST FOR THE HOLY GRAIL!
AND I! I, TOO, WILL GO!
YOU HAVE MADE ME VERY SAD. MANY OF YOU WILL NEVER RETURN FROM YOUR QUEST. NEVER AGAIN WILL WE ALL BE TOGETHER IN THIS WORLD. BUT YOUR QUEST IS GOOD, AND I KNOW THAT ONE OF YOU WILL FIND THE HOLY GRAIL.
THE NEXT DAY, THE KNIGHTS LEFT ON THEIR GREAT SEARCH, EACH GOING HIS SEPARATE WAY...

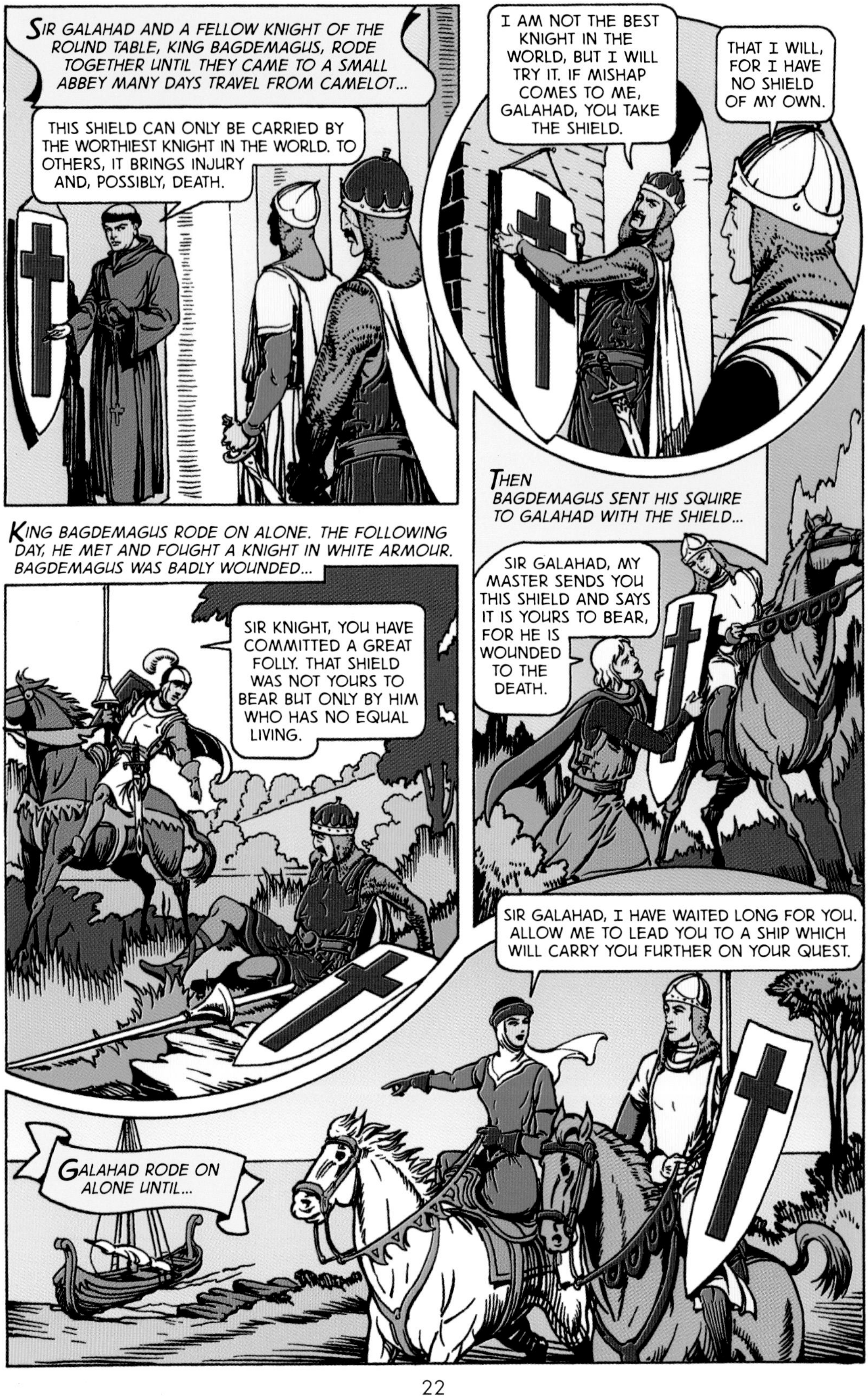
SIR GALAHAD AND A FELLOW KNIGHT OF THE ROUND TABLE, KING BAGDEMAGUS, RODE TOGETHER UNTIL THEY CAME TO A SMALL ABBEY MANY DAYS TRAVEL FROM CAMELOT...
THIS SHIELD CAN ONLY BE CARRIED BY THE WORTHIEST KNIGHT IN THE WORLD. TO OTHERS, IT BRINGS INJURY AND, POSSIBLY, DEATH.
I AM NOT THE BEST KNIGHT IN THE WORLD, BUT I WILL TRY IT. IF MISHAP COMES TO ME, GALAHAD, YOU TAKE THE SHIELD.
THAT I WILL, FOR I HAVE NO SHIELD OF MY OWN.
KING BAGDEMAGUS RODE ON ALONE. THE FOLLOWING DAY, HE MET AND FOUGHT A KNIGHT IN WHITE ARMOUR. BAGDEMAGUS WAS BADLY WOUNDED...
SIR KNIGHT, YOU HAVE COMMITTED A GREAT FOLLY. THAT SHIELD WAS NOT YOURS TO BEAR BUT ONLY BY HIM WHO HAS NO EQUAL LIVING.
THEN BAGDEMAGUS SENT HIS SQUIRE TO GALAHAD WITH THE SHIELD...
SIR GALAHAD, MY MASTER SENDS YOU THIS SHIELD AND SAYS IT IS YOURS TO BEAR, FOR HE IS WOUNDED TO THE DEATH.
GALAHAD RODE ON ALONE UNTIL...
SIR GALAHAD, I HAVE WAITED LONG FOR YOU. ALLOW ME TO LEAD YOU TO A SHIP WHICH WILL CARRY YOU FURTHER ON YOUR QUEST.

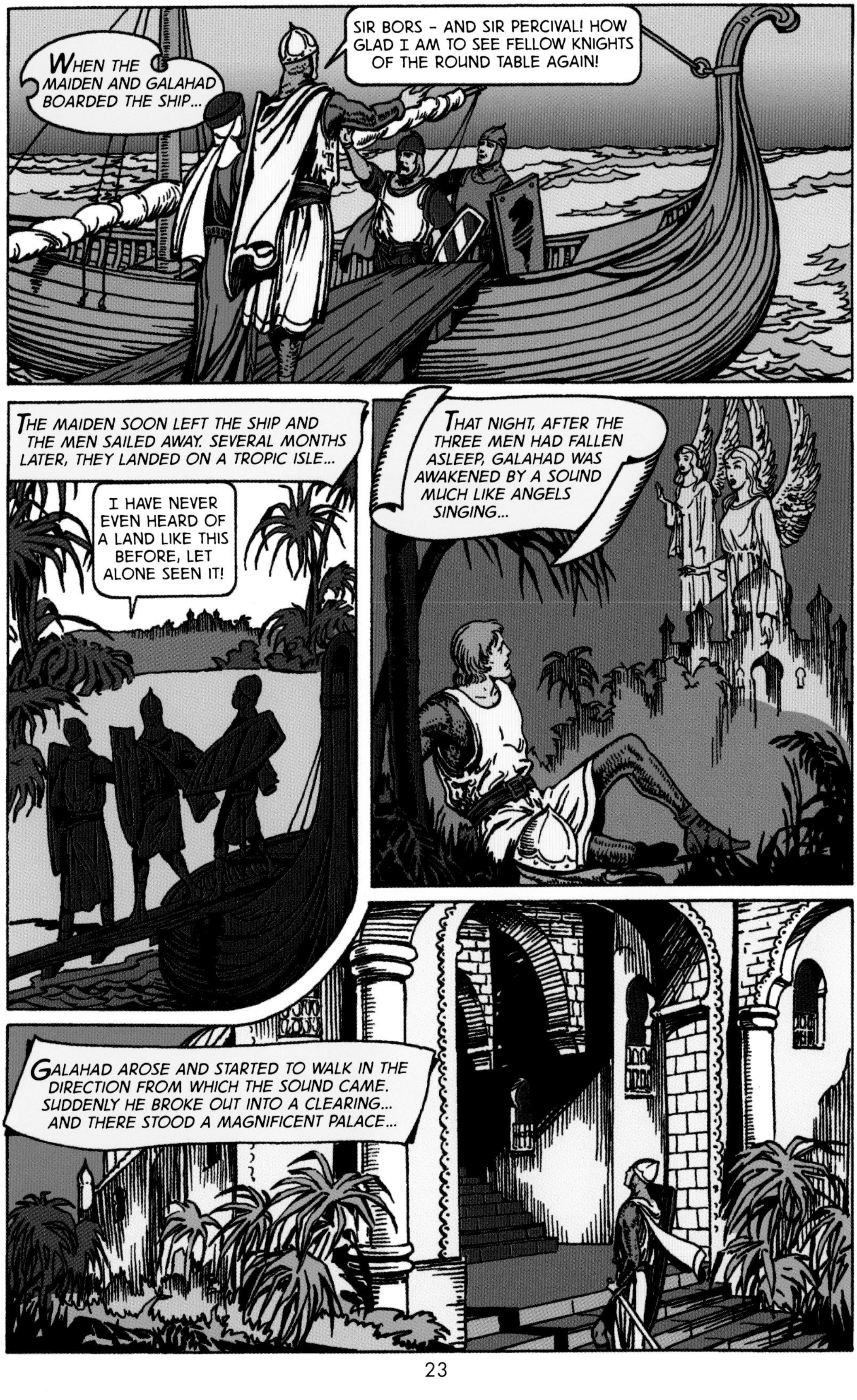
WHEN THE MAIDEN AND GALAHAD BOARDED THE SHIP...
SIR BORS - AND SIR PERCIVAL! HOW GLAD I AM TO SEE FELLOW KNIGHTS OF THE ROUND TABLE AGAIN!
THE MAIDEN SOON LEFT THE SHIP AND THE MEN SAILED AWAY. SEVERAL MONTHS LATER, THEY LANDED ON A TROPIC ISLE...
I HAVE NEVER EVEN HEARD OF A LAND LIKE THIS BEFORE, LET ALONE SEEN IT!
THAT NIGHT, AFTER THE THREE MEN HAD FALLEN ASLEEP, GALAHAD WAS AWAKENED BY A SOUND MUCH LIKE ANGELS SINGING...
GALAHAD AROSE AND STARTED TO WALK IN THE DIRECTION FROM WHICH THE SOUND CAME. SUDDENLY HE BROKE OUT INTO A CLEARING... AND THERE STOOD A MAGNIFICENT PALACE...

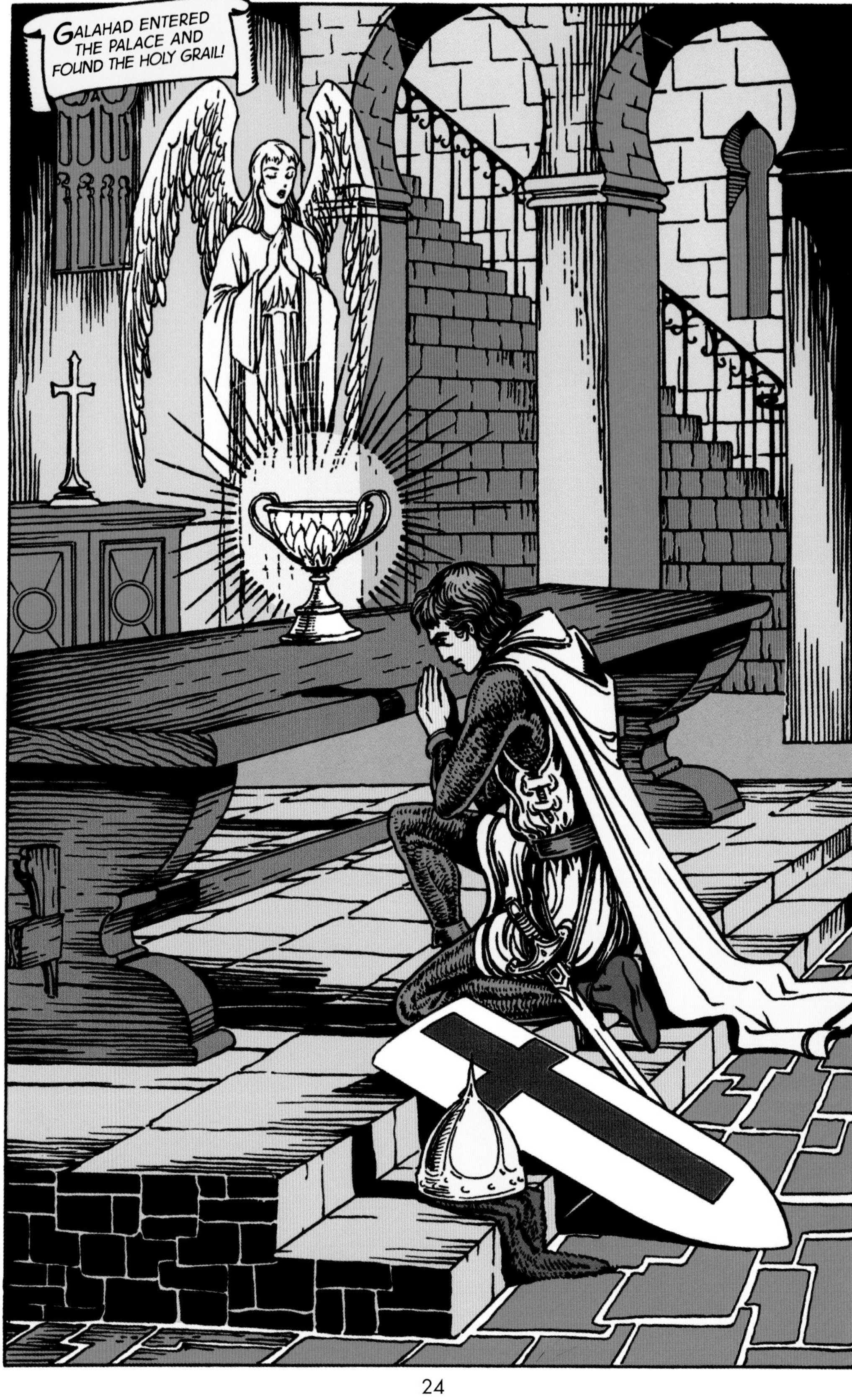
GALAHAD ENTERED THE PALACE AND FOUND THE HOLY GRAIL!

A FEW MOMENTS LATER, GALAHAD'S COMPANIONS ENTERED THE PALACE...

I TELL YOU, I SAW GALAHAD COME IN HERE JUST MINUTES AGO!

IT IS EMPTY! THE WHOLE PALACE IS DESERTED! BUT – BUT THAT IS GALAHAD'S HELMET!

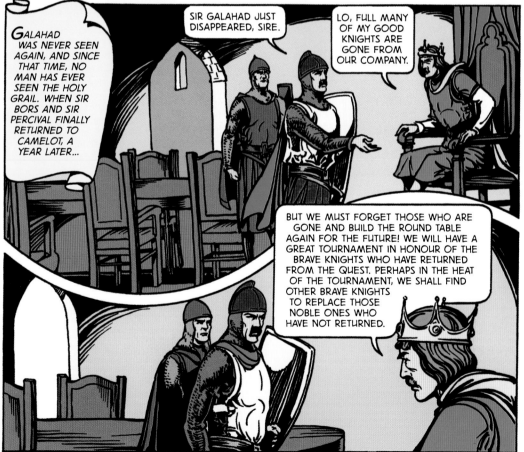

GALAHAD WAS NEVER SEEN AGAIN, AND SINCE THAT TIME, NO MAN HAS EVER SEEN THE HOLY GRAIL. WHEN SIR BORS AND SIR PERCIVAL FINALLY RETURNED TO CAMELOT, A YEAR LATER...

SIR GALAHAD JUST DISAPPEARED, SIRE.

LO, FULL MANY OF MY GOOD KNIGHTS ARE GONE FROM OUR COMPANY.

BUT WE MUST FORGET THOSE WHO ARE GONE AND BUILD THE ROUND TABLE AGAIN FOR THE FUTURE! WE WILL HAVE A GREAT TOURNAMENT IN HONOUR OF THE BRAVE KNIGHTS WHO HAVE RETURNED FROM THE QUEST. PERHAPS IN THE HEAT OF THE TOURNAMENT, WE SHALL FIND OTHER BRAVE KNIGHTS TO REPLACE THOSE NOBLE ONES WHO HAVE NOT RETURNED.

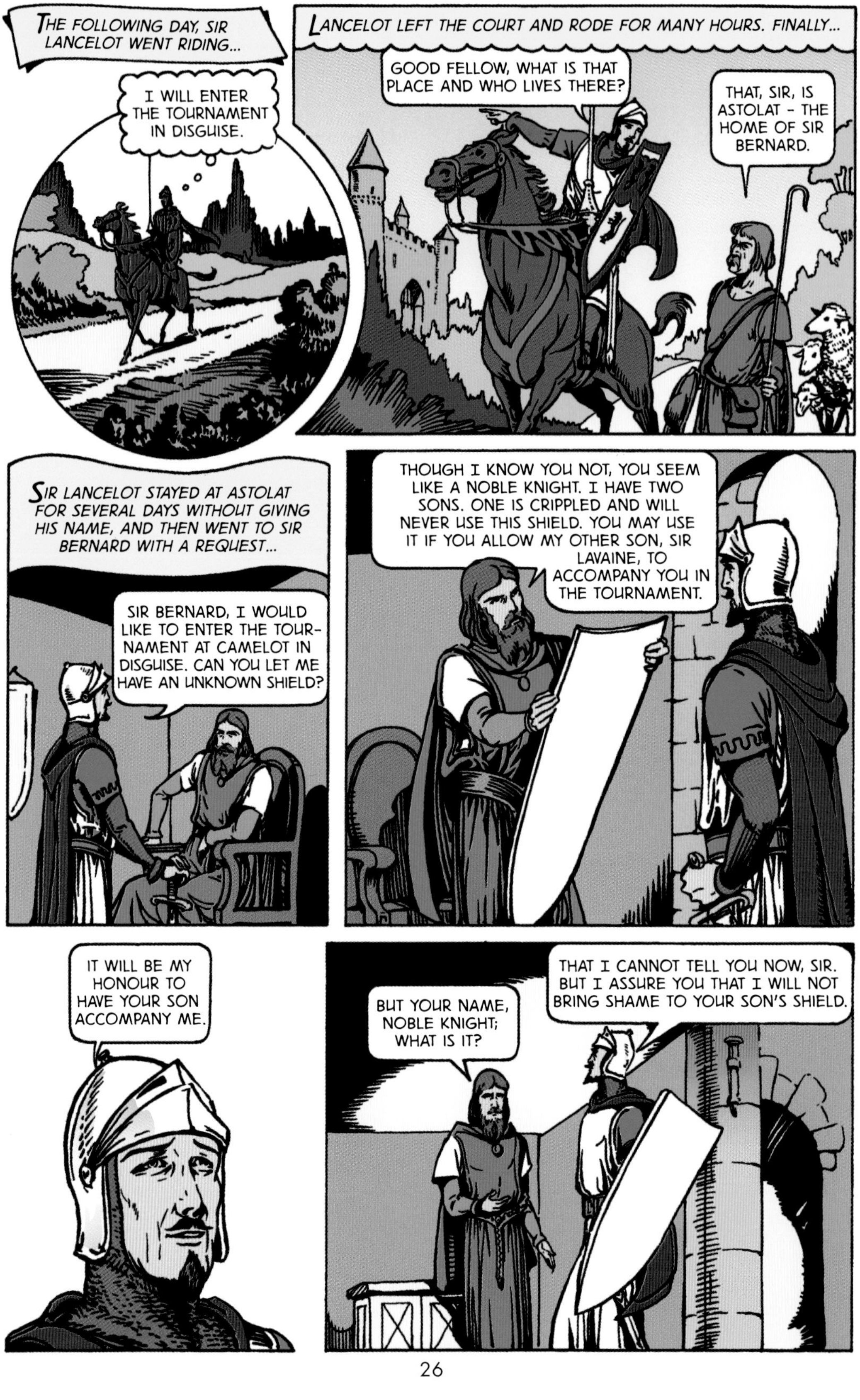
THE FOLLOWING DAY, SIR LANCELOT WENT RIDING...
I WILL ENTER THE TOURNAMENT IN DISGUISE.
LANCELOT LEFT THE COURT AND RODE FOR MANY HOURS. FINALLY...
GOOD FELLOW, WHAT IS THAT PLACE AND WHO LIVES THERE?
THAT, SIR, IS ASTOLAT – THE HOME OF SIR BERNARD.
SIR LANCELOT STAYED AT ASTOLAT FOR SEVERAL DAYS WITHOUT GIVING HIS NAME, AND THEN WENT TO SIR BERNARD WITH A REQUEST...
SIR BERNARD, I WOULD LIKE TO ENTER THE TOURNAMENT AT CAMELOT IN DISGUISE. CAN YOU LET ME HAVE AN UNKNOWN SHIELD?
THOUGH I KNOW YOU NOT, YOU SEEM LIKE A NOBLE KNIGHT. I HAVE TWO SONS. ONE IS CRIPPLED AND WILL NEVER USE THIS SHIELD. YOU MAY USE IT IF YOU ALLOW MY OTHER SON, SIR LAVAINE, TO ACCOMPANY YOU IN THE TOURNAMENT.
IT WILL BE MY HONOUR TO HAVE YOUR SON ACCOMPANY ME.
BUT YOUR NAME, NOBLE KNIGHT; WHAT IS IT?
THAT I CANNOT TELL YOU NOW, SIR. BUT I ASSURE YOU THAT I WILL NOT BRING SHAME TO YOUR SON'S SHIELD.

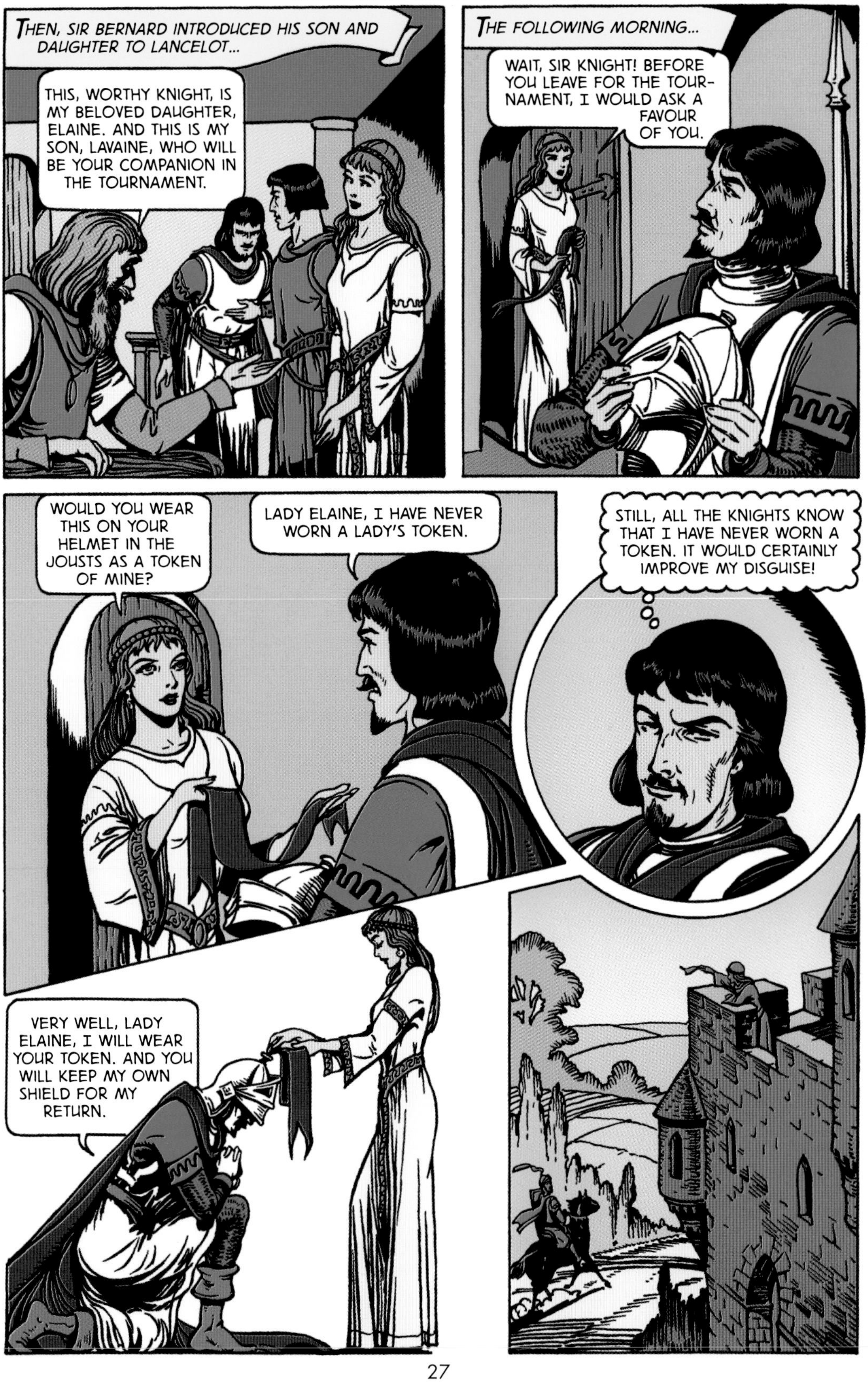
THEN, SIR BERNARD INTRODUCED HIS SON AND DAUGHTER TO LANCELOT...
THIS, WORTHY KNIGHT, IS MY BELOVED DAUGHTER, ELAINE. AND THIS IS MY SON, LAVAINE, WHO WILL BE YOUR COMPANION IN THE TOURNAMENT.
THE FOLLOWING MORNING...
WAIT, SIR KNIGHT! BEFORE YOU LEAVE FOR THE TOURNAMENT, I WOULD ASK A FAVOUR OF YOU.
WOULD YOU WEAR THIS ON YOUR HELMET IN THE JOUSTS AS A TOKEN OF MINE?
LADY ELAINE, I HAVE NEVER WORN A LADY'S TOKEN.
STILL, ALL THE KNIGHTS KNOW THAT I HAVE NEVER WORN A TOKEN. IT WOULD CERTAINLY IMPROVE MY DISGUISE!
VERY WELL, LADY ELAINE, I WILL WEAR YOUR TOKEN. AND YOU WILL KEEP MY OWN SHIELD FOR MY RETURN.

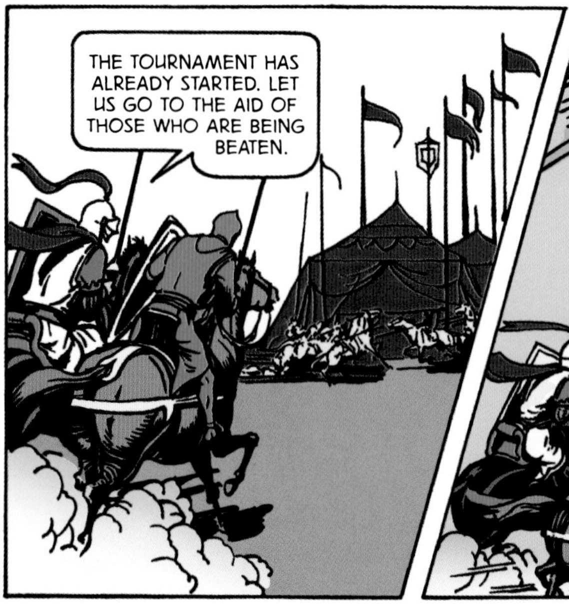
THE TOURNAMENT HAS ALREADY STARTED. LET US GO TO THE AID OF THOSE WHO ARE BEING BEATEN.

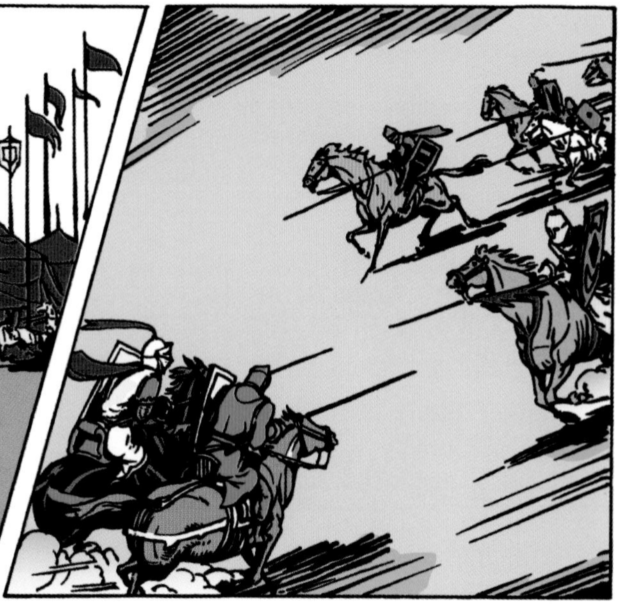

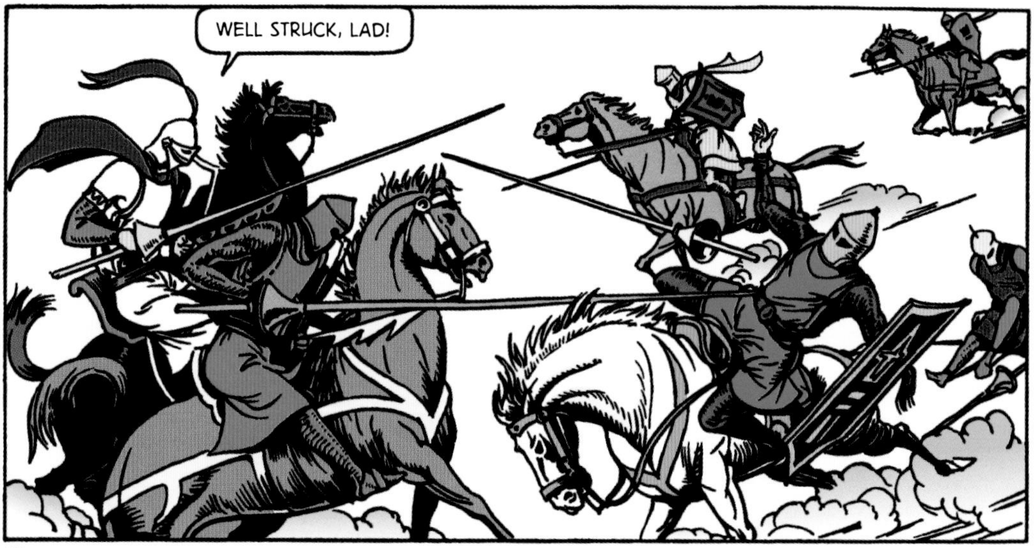
WELL STRUCK, LAD!

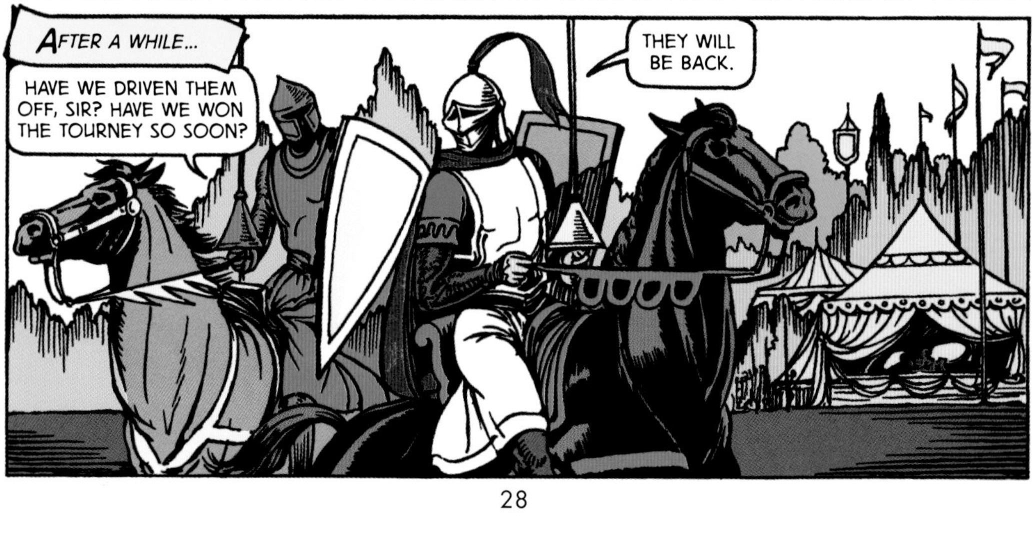
AFTER A WHILE...
HAVE WE DRIVEN THEM OFF, SIR? HAVE WE WON THE TOURNEY SO SOON?
THEY WILL BE BACK.

UNKNOWINGLY, LANCELOT HAD CHOSEN TO FIGHT AGAINST HIS COMRADES OF THE ROUND TABLE...

THOSE TWO KNIGHTS HAVE SHAMED US IN FRONT OF THE ENTIRE COURT.

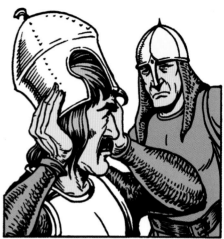

EXCEPT FOR THE RED SLEEVE ON HIS HELMET, I WOULD SAY THAT WAS LANCELOT. BUT HE HAS NEVER WORN A TOKEN FROM A LADY.

RUSH THEM IN A BODY!

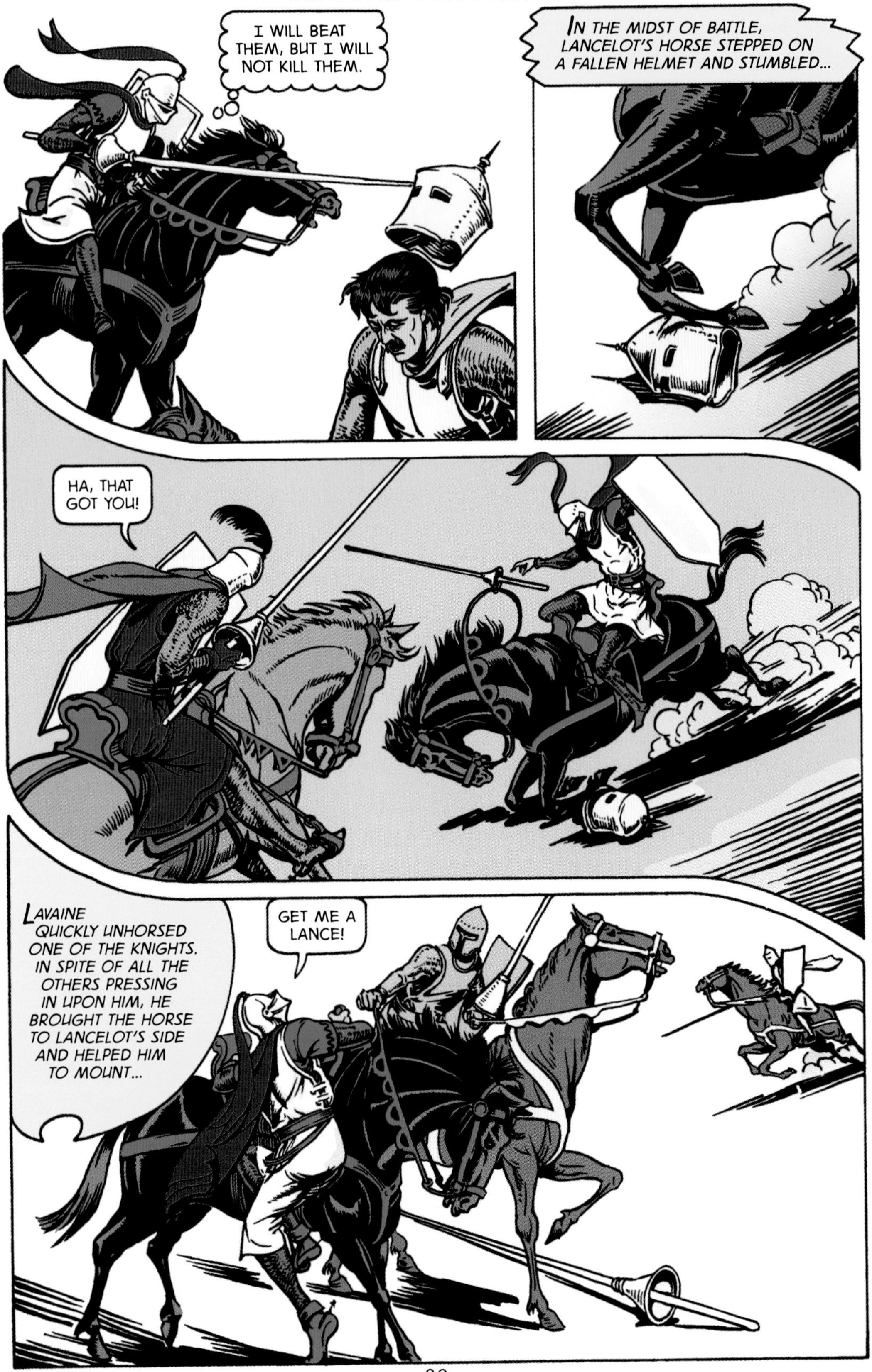
I WILL BEAT THEM, BUT I WILL NOT KILL THEM.
IN THE MIDST OF BATTLE, LANCELOT'S HORSE STEPPED ON A FALLEN HELMET AND STUMBLED...
HA, THAT GOT YOU!
LAVAINE QUICKLY UNHORSED ONE OF THE KNIGHTS. IN SPITE OF ALL THE OTHERS PRESSING IN UPON HIM, HE BROUGHT THE HORSE TO LANCELOT'S SIDE AND HELPED HIM TO MOUNT...
GET ME A LANCE!

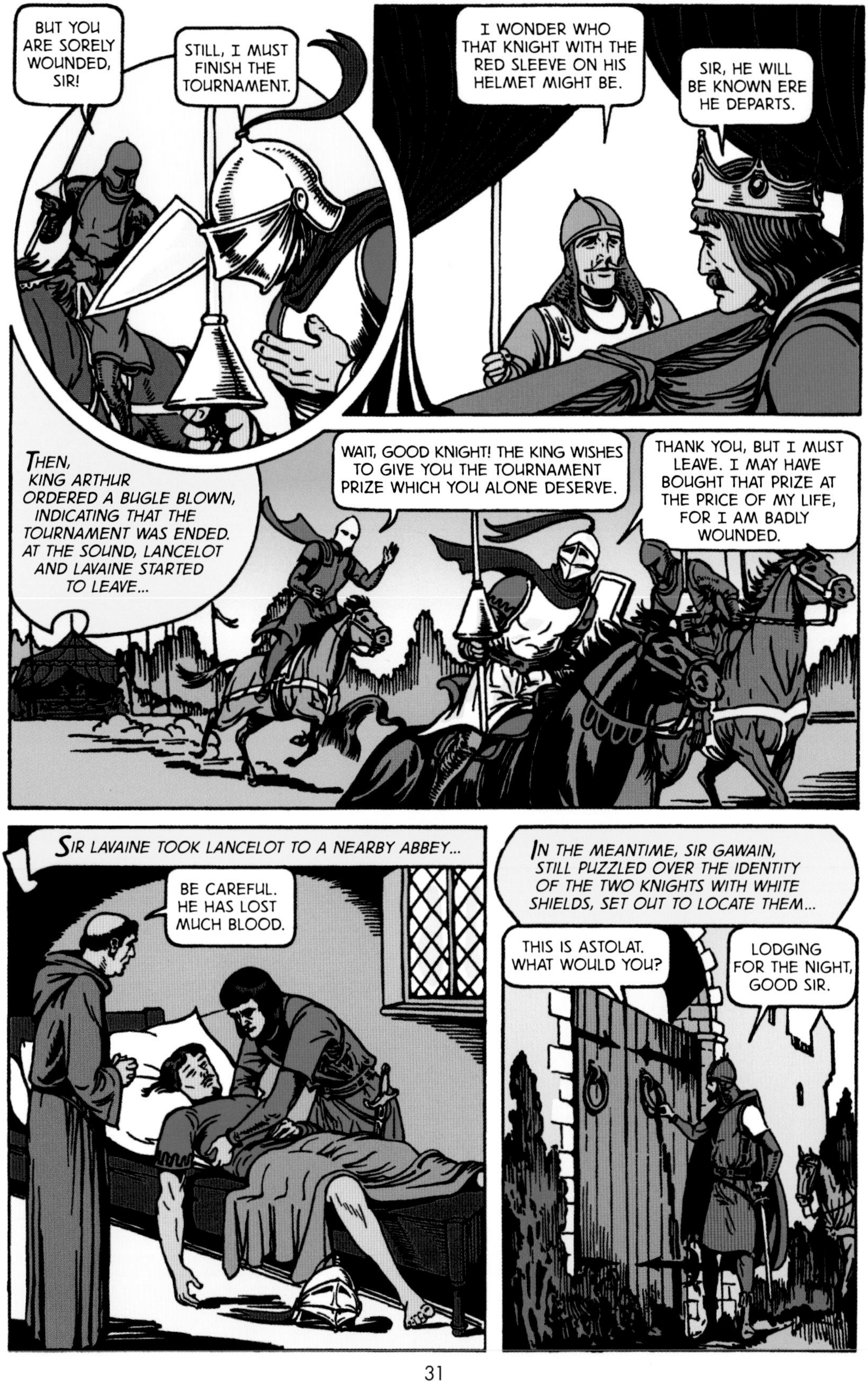

BUT YOU ARE SORELY WOUNDED, SIR!
STILL, I MUST FINISH THE TOURNAMENT.
I WONDER WHO THAT KNIGHT WITH THE RED SLEEVE ON HIS HELMET MIGHT BE.
SIR, HE WILL BE KNOWN ERE HE DEPARTS.
THEN, KING ARTHUR ORDERED A BUGLE BLOWN, INDICATING THAT THE TOURNAMENT WAS ENDED. AT THE SOUND, LANCELOT AND LAVAINE STARTED TO LEAVE...
WAIT, GOOD KNIGHT! THE KING WISHES TO GIVE YOU THE TOURNAMENT PRIZE WHICH YOU ALONE DESERVE.
THANK YOU, BUT I MUST LEAVE. I MAY HAVE BOUGHT THAT PRIZE AT THE PRICE OF MY LIFE, FOR I AM BADLY WOUNDED.
SIR LAVAINE TOOK LANCELOT TO A NEARBY ABBEY...
BE CAREFUL. HE HAS LOST MUCH BLOOD.
IN THE MEANTIME, SIR GAWAIN, STILL PUZZLED OVER THE IDENTITY OF THE TWO KNIGHTS WITH WHITE SHIELDS, SET OUT TO LOCATE THEM...
THIS IS ASTOLAT. WHAT WOULD YOU?
LODGING FOR THE NIGHT, GOOD SIR.

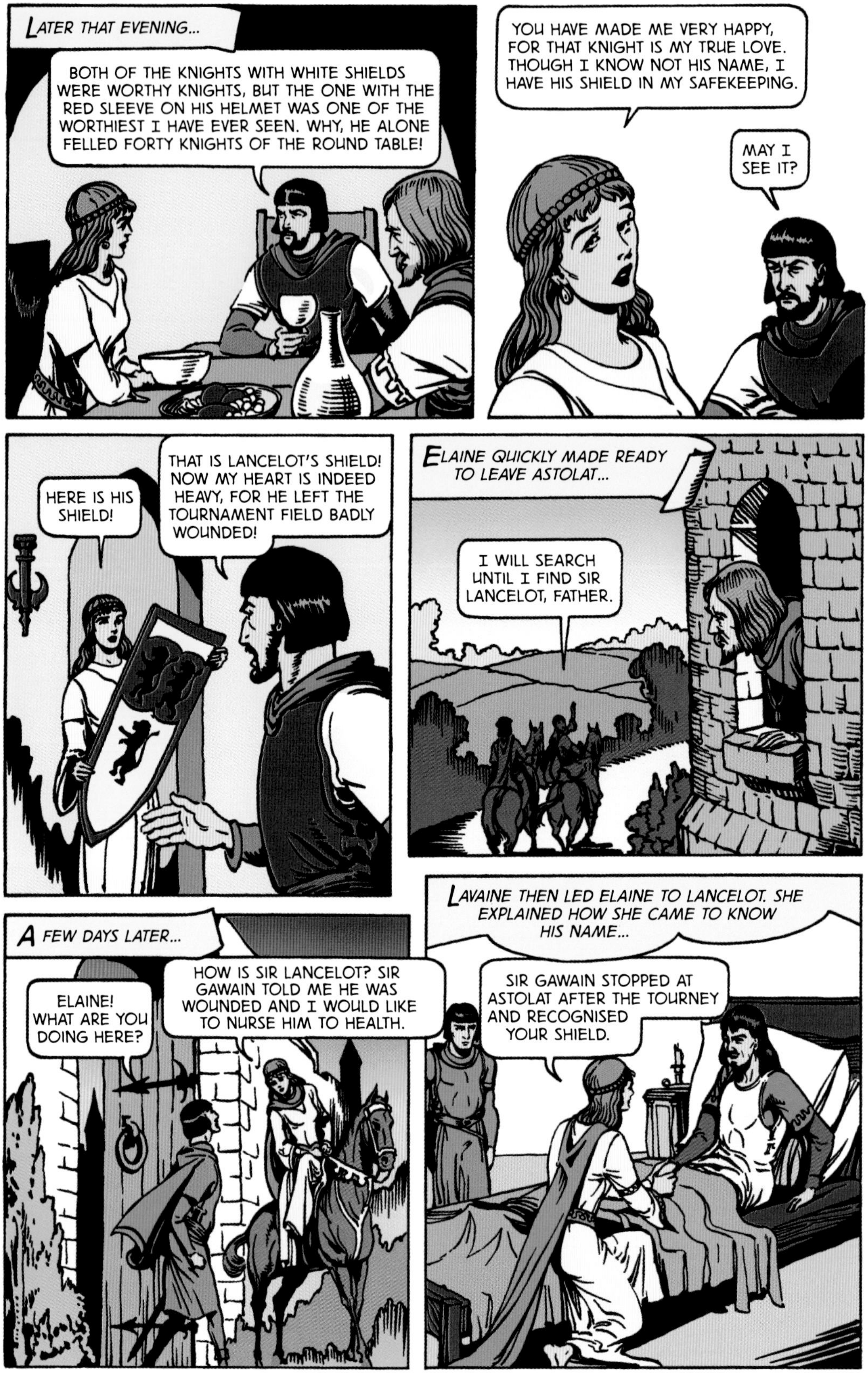
LATER THAT EVENING...
BOTH OF THE KNIGHTS WITH WHITE SHIELDS WERE WORTHY KNIGHTS, BUT THE ONE WITH THE RED SLEEVE ON HIS HELMET WAS ONE OF THE WORTHIEST I HAVE EVER SEEN. WHY, HE ALONE FELLED FORTY KNIGHTS OF THE ROUND TABLE!
YOU HAVE MADE ME VERY HAPPY, FOR THAT KNIGHT IS MY TRUE LOVE. THOUGH I KNOW NOT HIS NAME, I HAVE HIS SHIELD IN MY SAFEKEEPING.
MAY I SEE IT?
HERE IS HIS SHIELD!
THAT IS LANCELOT'S SHIELD! NOW MY HEART IS INDEED HEAVY, FOR HE LEFT THE TOURNAMENT FIELD BADLY WOUNDED!
ELAINE QUICKLY MADE READY TO LEAVE ASTOLAT...
I WILL SEARCH UNTIL I FIND SIR LANCELOT, FATHER.
A FEW DAYS LATER...
ELAINE! WHAT ARE YOU DOING HERE?
HOW IS SIR LANCELOT? SIR GAWAIN TOLD ME HE WAS WOUNDED AND I WOULD LIKE TO NURSE HIM TO HEALTH.
LAVAINE THEN LED ELAINE TO LANCELOT. SHE EXPLAINED HOW SHE CAME TO KNOW HIS NAME...
SIR GAWAIN STOPPED AT ASTOLAT AFTER THE TOURNEY AND RECOGNISED YOUR SHIELD.

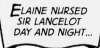

ELAINE NURSED SIR LANCELOT DAY AND NIGHT...

YOUR TENDER CARE HAS WORKED WONDERS, FAIR LADY. SOON WE SHALL BE ABLE TO RETURN TO ASTOLAT.

A FEW MONTHS LATER, AT ASTOLAT...

SOON YOU RETURN TO KING ARTHUR'S COURT. KNOW FIRST THAT I HAVE NEVER LOVED ANY MAN BUT YOU AND I WILL LOVE NO OTHER.

FAIR LADY, I VOWED NEVER TO WED. FORGET ME AND FIND SOME GOOD KNIGHT TO WED AND I WILL SETTLE A THOUSAND POUNDS YEARLY ON YOU.

I WILL DIE BEFORE I FORGET YOU.

SHORTLY AFTER LANCELOT RETURNED TO CAMELOT...

SHE WILL NOT EAT AND DOES NOT SLEEP.

I AM SORRY, SIR BERNARD, BUT I FIND NOTHING WRONG WITH HER PHYSICALLY.

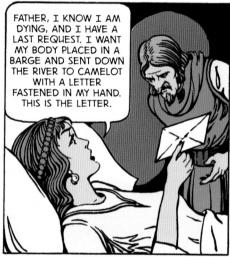

FATHER, I KNOW I AM DYING, AND I HAVE A LAST REQUEST. I WANT MY BODY PLACED IN A BARGE AND SENT DOWN THE RIVER TO CAMELOT WITH A LETTER FASTENED IN MY HAND. THIS IS THE LETTER.

A FEW NIGHTS LATER, ELAINE DIED.

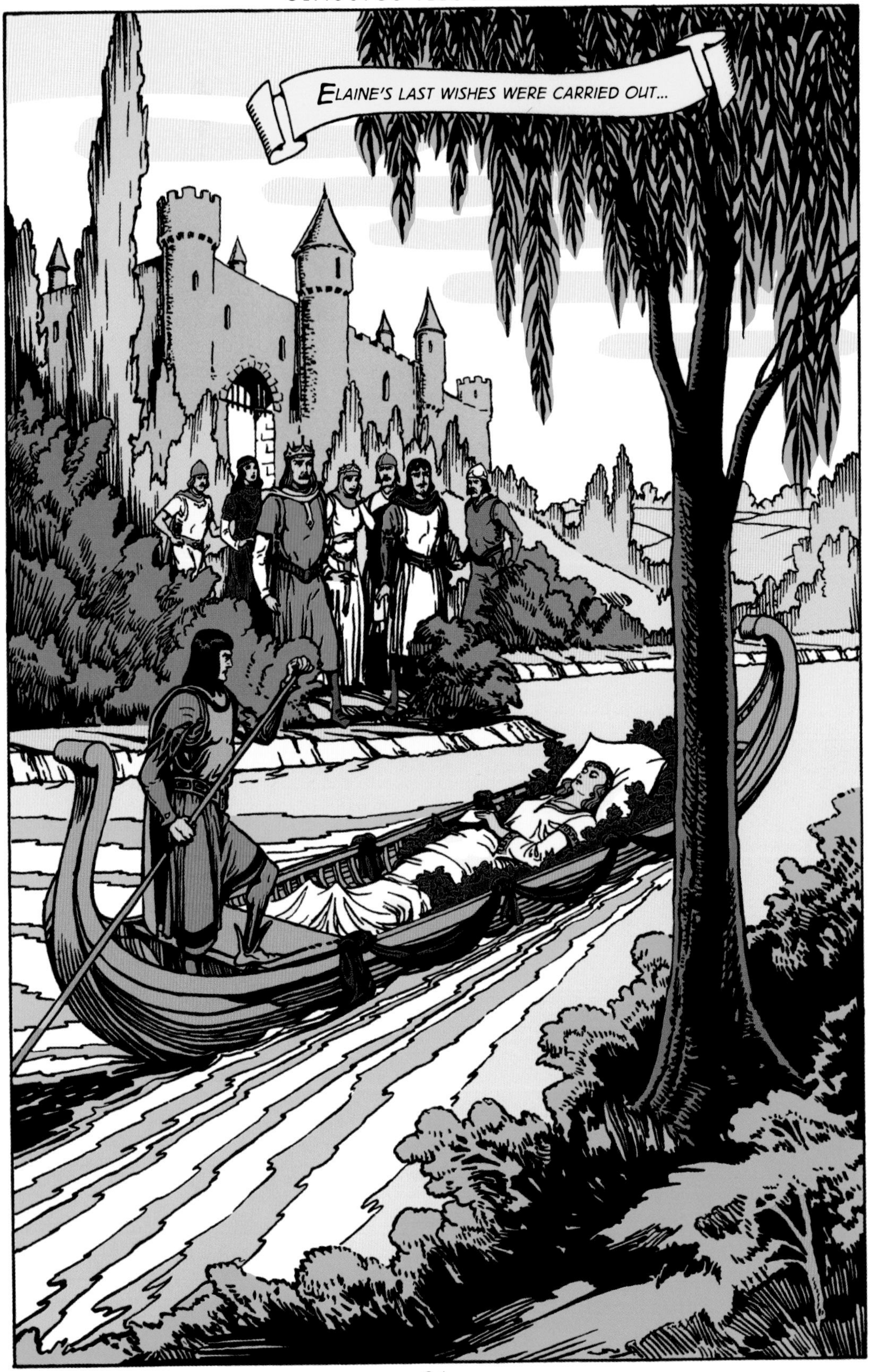
ELAINE'S LAST WISHES WERE CARRIED OUT...

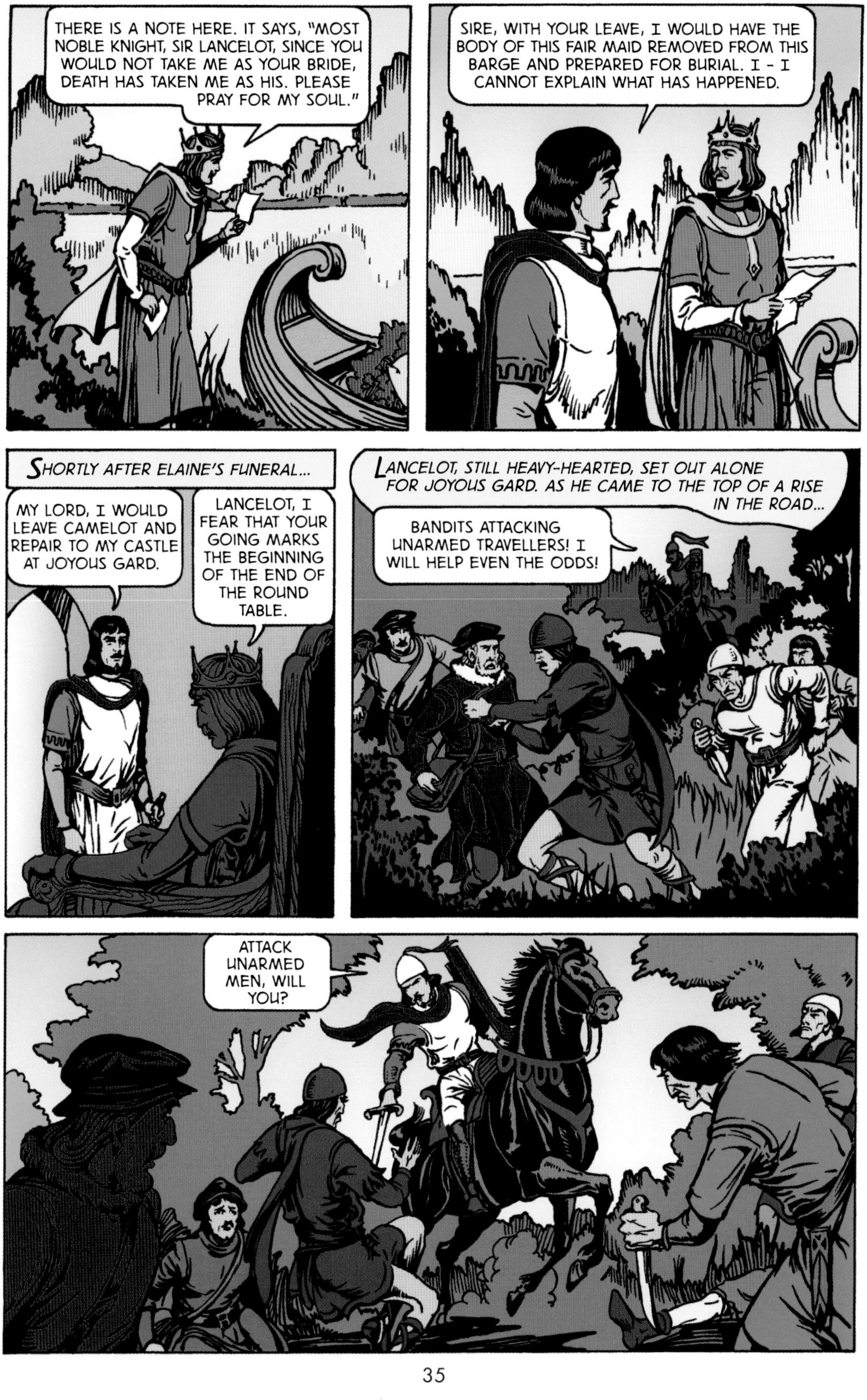
THERE IS A NOTE HERE. IT SAYS, "MOST NOBLE KNIGHT, SIR LANCELOT, SINCE YOU WOULD NOT TAKE ME AS YOUR BRIDE, DEATH HAS TAKEN ME AS HIS. PLEASE PRAY FOR MY SOUL."
SIRE, WITH YOUR LEAVE, I WOULD HAVE THE BODY OF THIS FAIR MAID REMOVED FROM THIS BARGE AND PREPARED FOR BURIAL. I - I CANNOT EXPLAIN WHAT HAS HAPPENED.
SHORTLY AFTER ELAINE'S FUNERAL...
MY LORD, I WOULD LEAVE CAMELOT AND REPAIR TO MY CASTLE AT JOYOUS GARD.
LANCELOT, I FEAR THAT YOUR GOING MARKS THE BEGINNING OF THE END OF THE ROUND TABLE.
LANCELOT, STILL HEAVY-HEARTED, SET OUT ALONE FOR JOYOUS GARD. AS HE CAME TO THE TOP OF A RISE IN THE ROAD...
BANDITS ATTACKING UNARMED TRAVELLERS! I WILL HELP EVEN THE ODDS!
ATTACK UNARMED MEN, WILL YOU?

IN THE DARKNESS, LANCELOT KILLED SEVERAL MEN. THEN...

COWARDS! ARE YE AFRAID TO FACE THE STEEL OF AN ARMED MAN?

LANCELOT CHASED THEM A WHILE AND THEN WENT ON HIS WAY. HOWEVER, BACK AT THE ROAD...

OUR FRIENDS, SIR GAHERIS AND SIR GARETH, HAVE BEEN SLAIN BY THE KNIGHT WHO PRETENDED TO HELP US. I RECOGNISED HIS SHIELD. IT WAS SIR LANCELOT.

IF HE DID, IT WAS AN ACCIDENT.

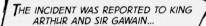

THE INCIDENT WAS REPORTED TO KING ARTHUR AND SIR GAWAIN...

...AND THAT IS HOW SIR GAWAIN'S BROTHERS, SIR GARETH AND SIR GAHERIS, WERE KILLED. SIR LANCELOT DID IT. I SAW IT.

SIRE, YOU HEARD HIM. LANCELOT KILLED MY BROTHERS WHEN THEY WERE UNARMED! I SWEAR I WILL NOT REST UNTIL THEY ARE AVENGED!

ARTHUR WITHSTOOD GAWAIN'S PLEAS TO MAKE WAR ON LANCELOT. SOMETIME LATER...

GAWAIN KEEPS INSISTING THAT LANCELOT AT LEAST COME BACK TO COURT AND EXPLAIN WHAT HAPPENED. I HAVE SENT A MESSAGE, ASKING HIM TO RETURN.

A MONTH LATER...

SIRE, LANCELOT HAS NOT ANSWERED. THAT PROVES HIS GUILT. I DEMAND THAT HE BE PUNISHED!

VERY WELL, I WILL TAKE AN ARMY TO JOYOUS GARD AND BRING HIM BACK.

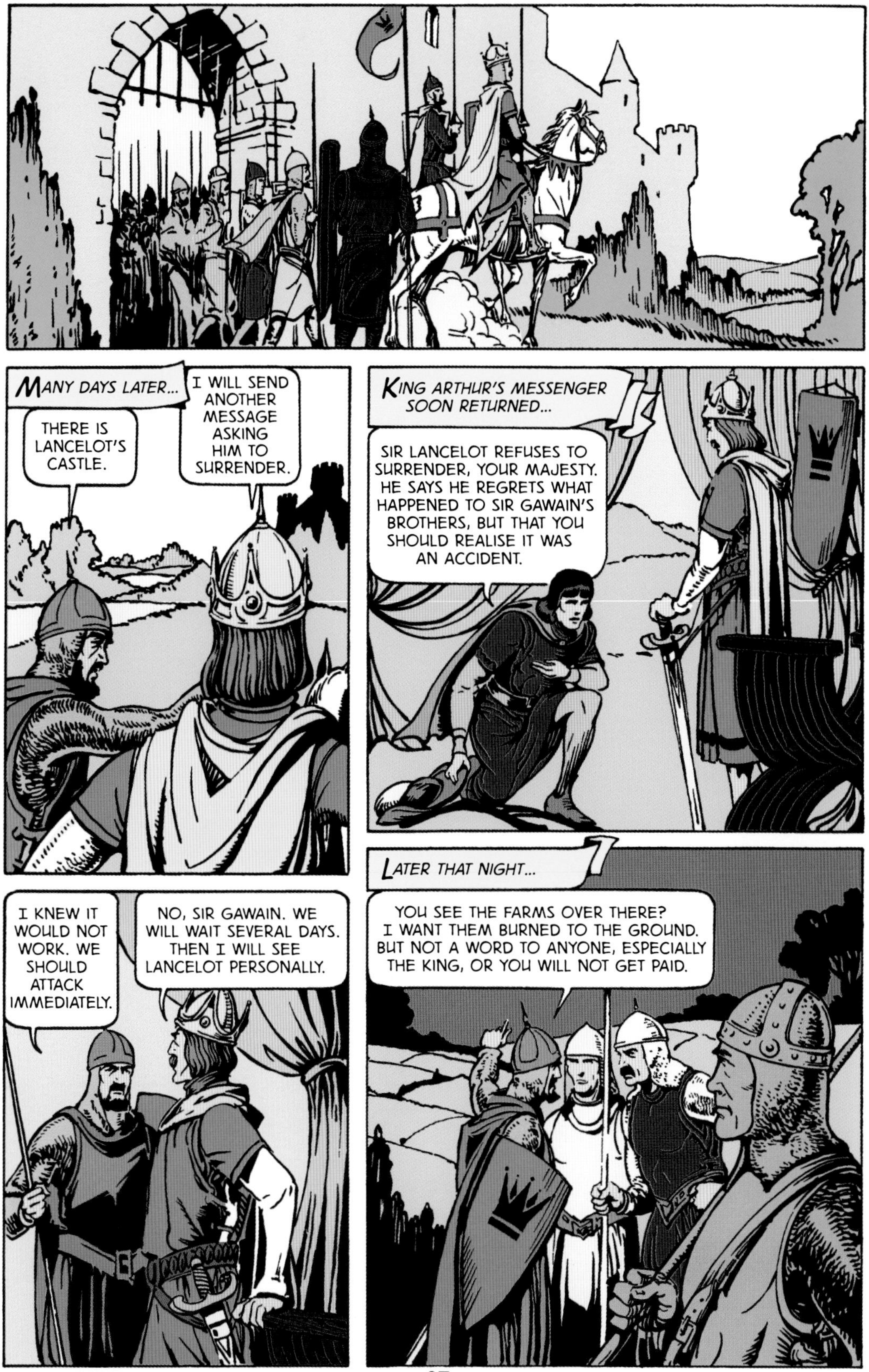
MANY DAYS LATER...
THERE IS LANCELOT'S CASTLE.
I WILL SEND ANOTHER MESSAGE ASKING HIM TO SURRENDER.
KING ARTHUR'S MESSENGER SOON RETURNED...
SIR LANCELOT REFUSES TO SURRENDER, YOUR MAJESTY. HE SAYS HE REGRETS WHAT HAPPENED TO SIR GAWAIN'S BROTHERS, BUT THAT YOU SHOULD REALISE IT WAS AN ACCIDENT.
I KNEW IT WOULD NOT WORK. WE SHOULD ATTACK IMMEDIATELY.
NO, SIR GAWAIN. WE WILL WAIT SEVERAL DAYS. THEN I WILL SEE LANCELOT PERSONALLY.
LATER THAT NIGHT...
YOU SEE THE FARMS OVER THERE? I WANT THEM BURNED TO THE GROUND. BUT NOT A WORD TO ANYONE, ESPECIALLY THE KING, OR YOU WILL NOT GET PAID.

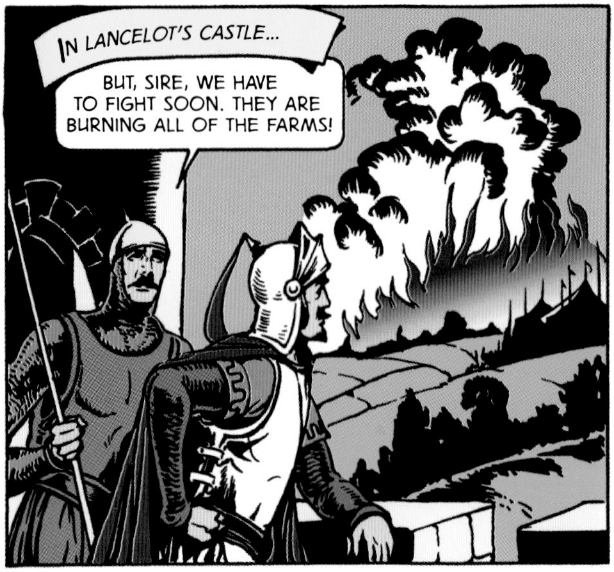
IN LANCELOT'S CASTLE...
BUT, SIRE, WE HAVE TO FIGHT SOON. THEY ARE BURNING ALL OF THE FARMS!

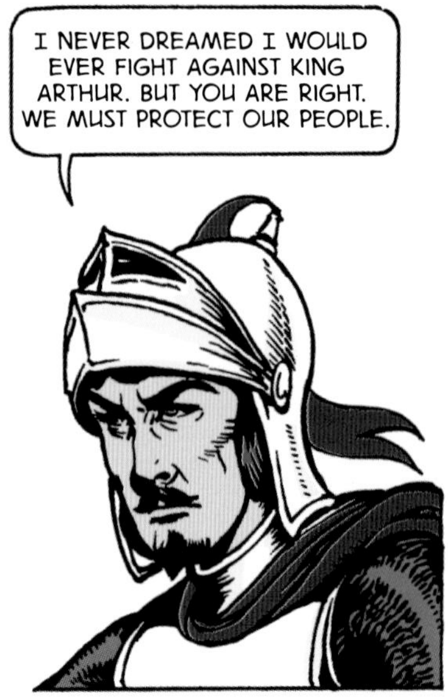
I NEVER DREAMED I WOULD EVER FIGHT AGAINST KING ARTHUR. BUT YOU ARE RIGHT. WE MUST PROTECT OUR PEOPLE.

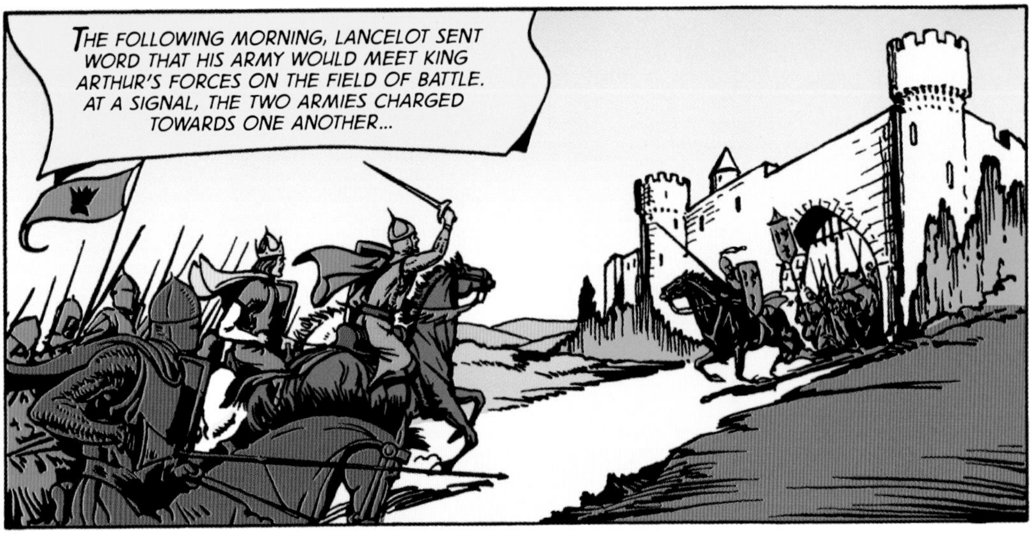
THE FOLLOWING MORNING, LANCELOT SENT WORD THAT HIS ARMY WOULD MEET KING ARTHUR'S FORCES ON THE FIELD OF BATTLE. AT A SIGNAL, THE TWO ARMIES CHARGED TOWARDS ONE ANOTHER...

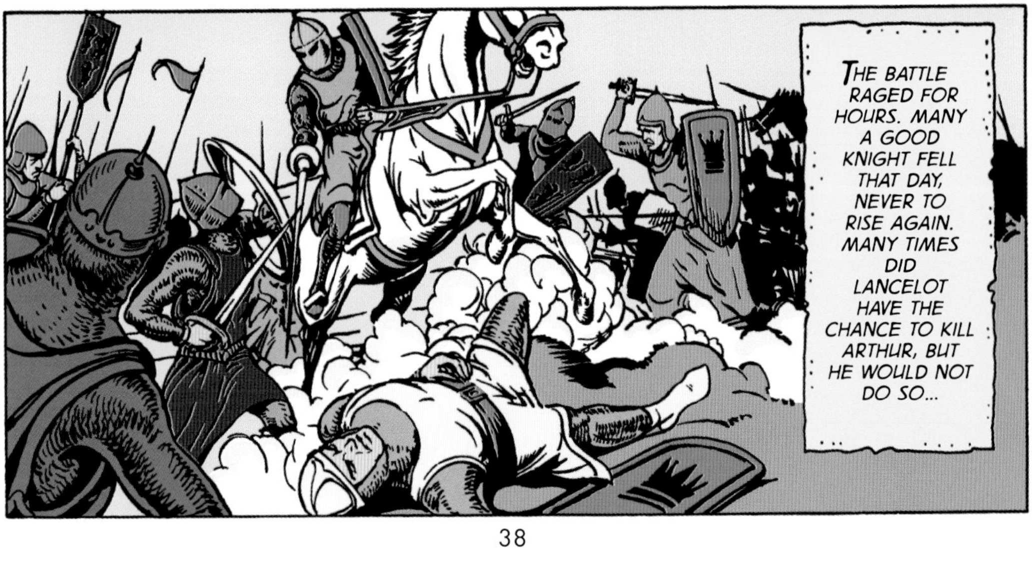
THE BATTLE RAGED FOR HOURS. MANY A GOOD KNIGHT FELL THAT DAY, NEVER TO RISE AGAIN. MANY TIMES DID LANCELOT HAVE THE CHANCE TO KILL ARTHUR, BUT HE WOULD NOT DO SO...

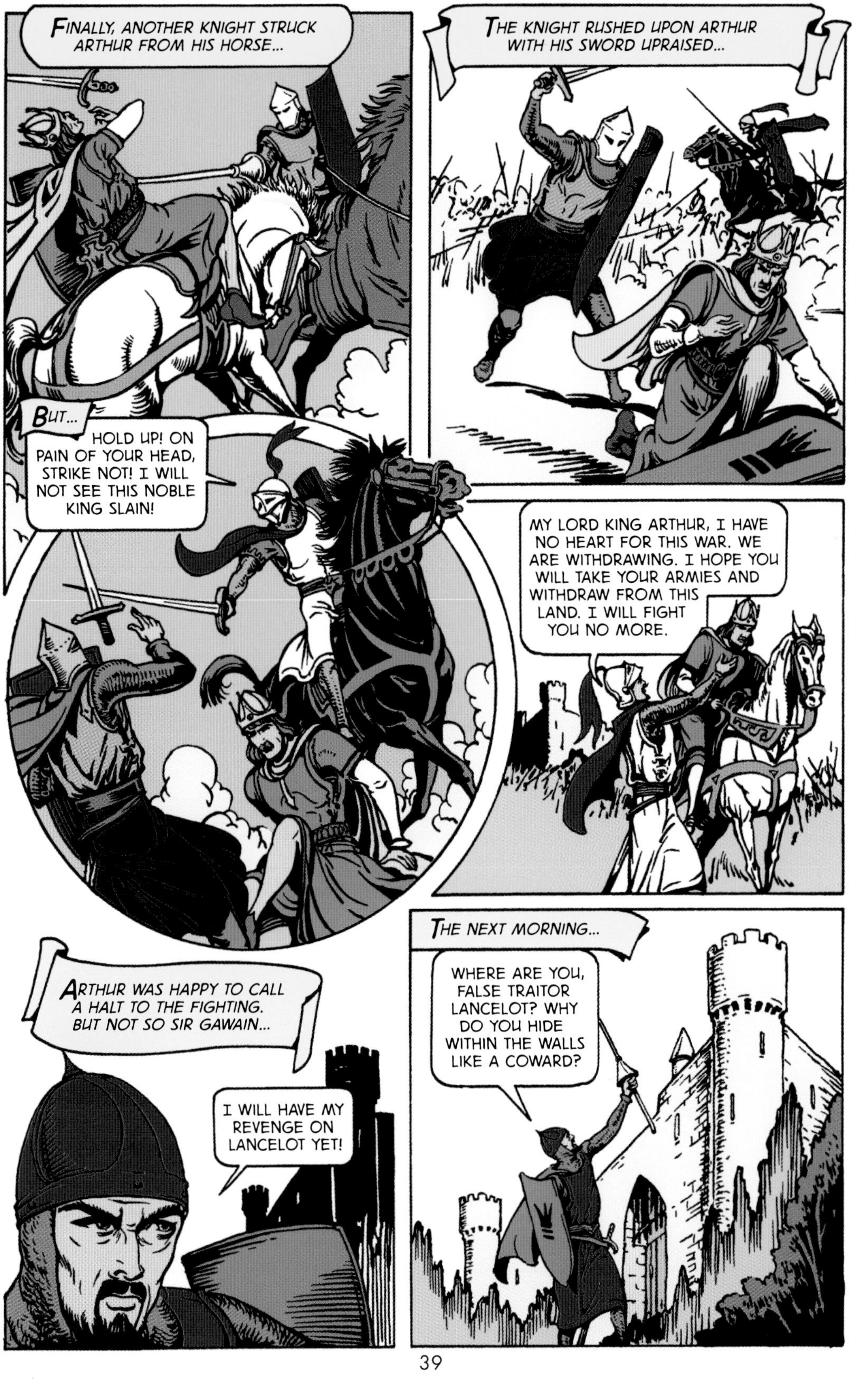
FINALLY, ANOTHER KNIGHT STRUCK ARTHUR FROM HIS HORSE...
THE KNIGHT RUSHED UPON ARTHUR WITH HIS SWORD UPRAISED...
BUT...
HOLD UP! ON PAIN OF YOUR HEAD, STRIKE NOT! I WILL NOT SEE THIS NOBLE KING SLAIN!
MY LORD KING ARTHUR, I HAVE NO HEART FOR THIS WAR. WE ARE WITHDRAWING. I HOPE YOU WILL TAKE YOUR ARMIES AND WITHDRAW FROM THIS LAND. I WILL FIGHT YOU NO MORE.
ARTHUR WAS HAPPY TO CALL A HALT TO THE FIGHTING. BUT NOT SO SIR GAWAIN...
I WILL HAVE MY REVENGE ON LANCELOT YET!
THE NEXT MORNING...
WHERE ARE YOU, FALSE TRAITOR LANCELOT? WHY DO YOU HIDE WITHIN THE WALLS LIKE A COWARD?

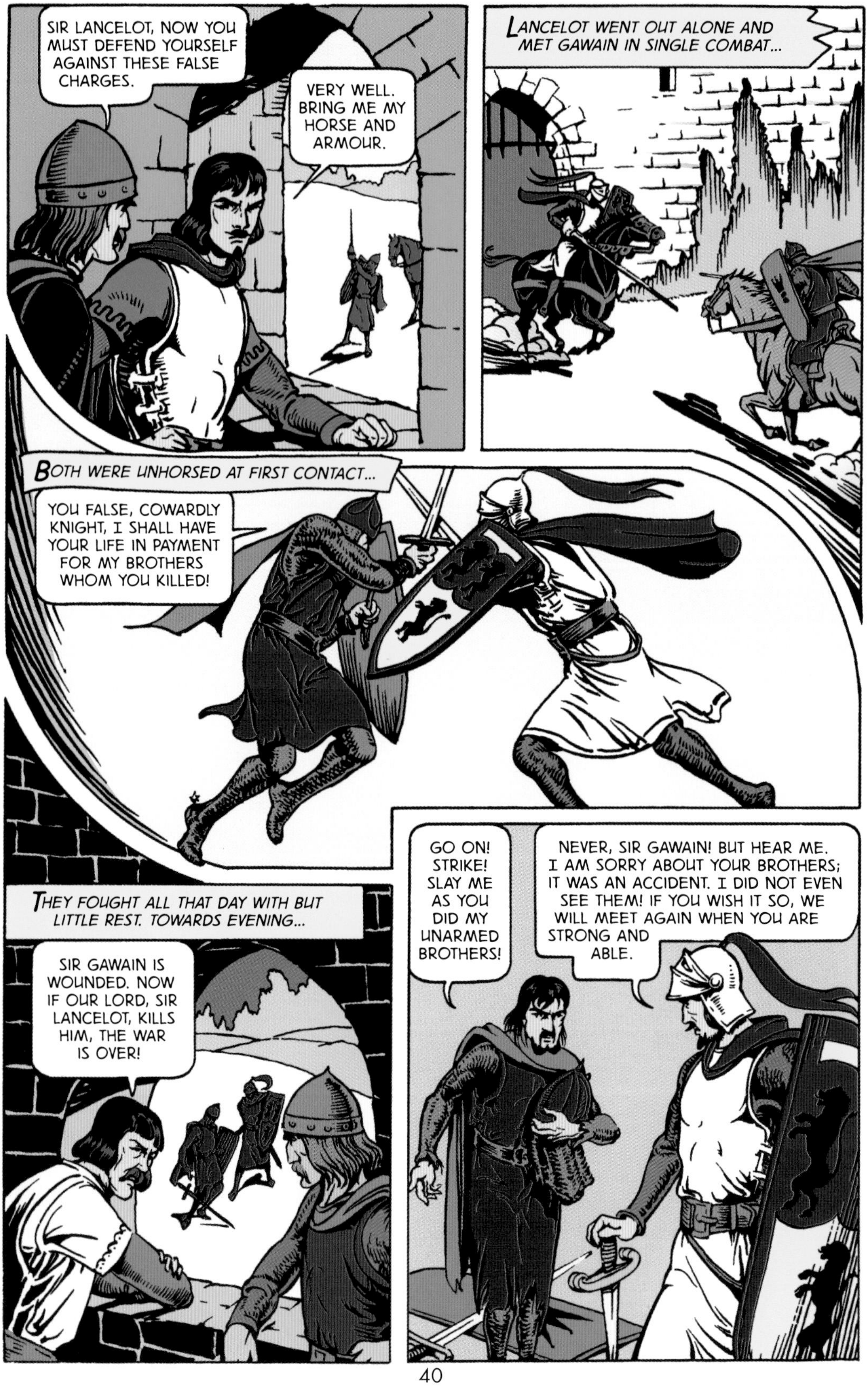
SIR LANCELOT, NOW YOU MUST DEFEND YOURSELF AGAINST THESE FALSE CHARGES.
VERY WELL. BRING ME MY HORSE AND ARMOUR.
LANCELOT WENT OUT ALONE AND MET GAWAIN IN SINGLE COMBAT...
BOTH WERE UNHORSED AT FIRST CONTACT...
YOU FALSE, COWARDLY KNIGHT, I SHALL HAVE YOUR LIFE IN PAYMENT FOR MY BROTHERS WHOM YOU KILLED!
THEY FOUGHT ALL THAT DAY WITH BUT LITTLE REST. TOWARDS EVENING...
SIR GAWAIN IS WOUNDED. NOW IF OUR LORD, SIR LANCELOT, KILLS HIM, THE WAR IS OVER!
GO ON! STRIKE! SLAY ME AS YOU DID MY UNARMED BROTHERS!
NEVER, SIR GAWAIN! BUT HEAR ME. I AM SORRY ABOUT YOUR BROTHERS; IT WAS AN ACCIDENT. I DID NOT EVEN SEE THEM! IF YOU WISH IT SO, WE WILL MEET AGAIN WHEN YOU ARE STRONG AND ABLE.

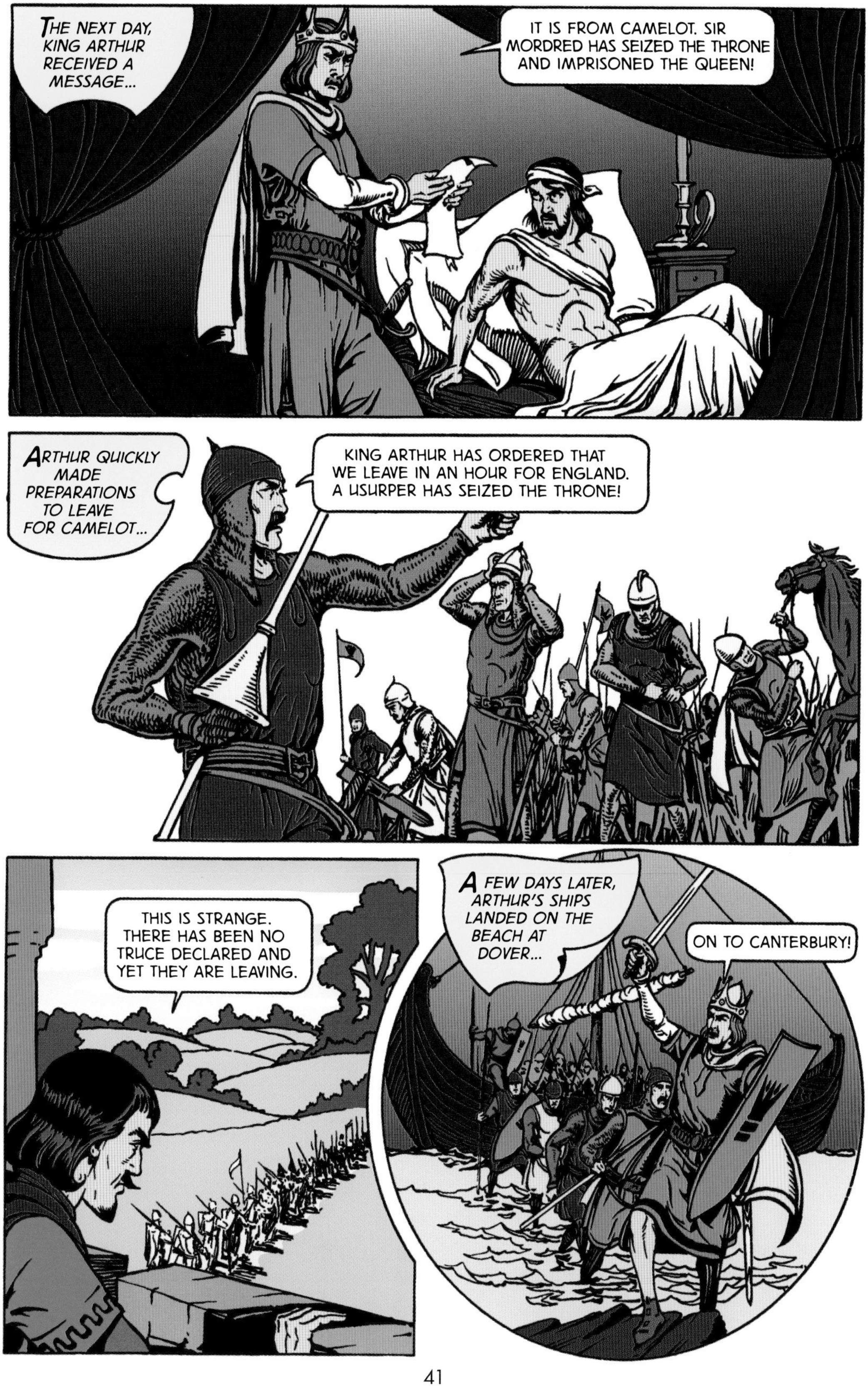
THE NEXT DAY, KING ARTHUR RECEIVED A MESSAGE...
IT IS FROM CAMELOT. SIR MORDRED HAS SEIZED THE THRONE AND IMPRISONED THE QUEEN!
ARTHUR QUICKLY MADE PREPARATIONS TO LEAVE FOR CAMELOT...
KING ARTHUR HAS ORDERED THAT WE LEAVE IN AN HOUR FOR ENGLAND. A USURPER HAS SEIZED THE THRONE!
THIS IS STRANGE. THERE HAS BEEN NO TRUCE DECLARED AND YET THEY ARE LEAVING.
A FEW DAYS LATER, ARTHUR'S SHIPS LANDED ON THE BEACH AT DOVER...
ON TO CANTERBURY!

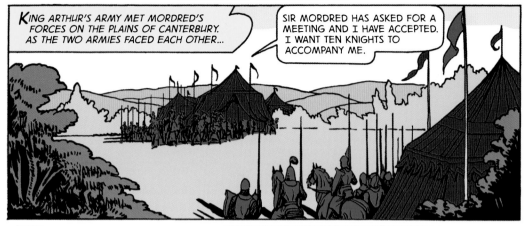

KING ARTHUR'S ARMY MET MORDRED'S FORCES ON THE PLAINS OF CANTERBURY. AS THE TWO ARMIES FACED EACH OTHER...

SIR MORDRED HAS ASKED FOR A MEETING AND I HAVE ACCEPTED. I WANT TEN KNIGHTS TO ACCOMPANY ME.

MORDRED MAY INTEND SOME TREACHERY. IF YOU SEE ONE SWORD DRAWN, ATTACK WITHOUT DELAY!

AT THE SAME TIME...

KING ARTHUR IS AN HONOURABLE MAN, BUT I DO NOT TRUST SOME OF HIS KNIGHTS, SO I TOLD OUR MEN TO ATTACK IF THEY SEE A SINGLE SWORD DRAWN.

UNFORTUNATELY, JUST AS ARTHUR AND MORDRED HAD COME TO PEACEFUL TERMS...

LOOK OUT! A SNAKE!

THE UPRAISED SWORD WAS SIGHTED BY BOTH ARMIES AND THEY CHARGED TOWARDS ONE ANOTHER INSTANTLY...

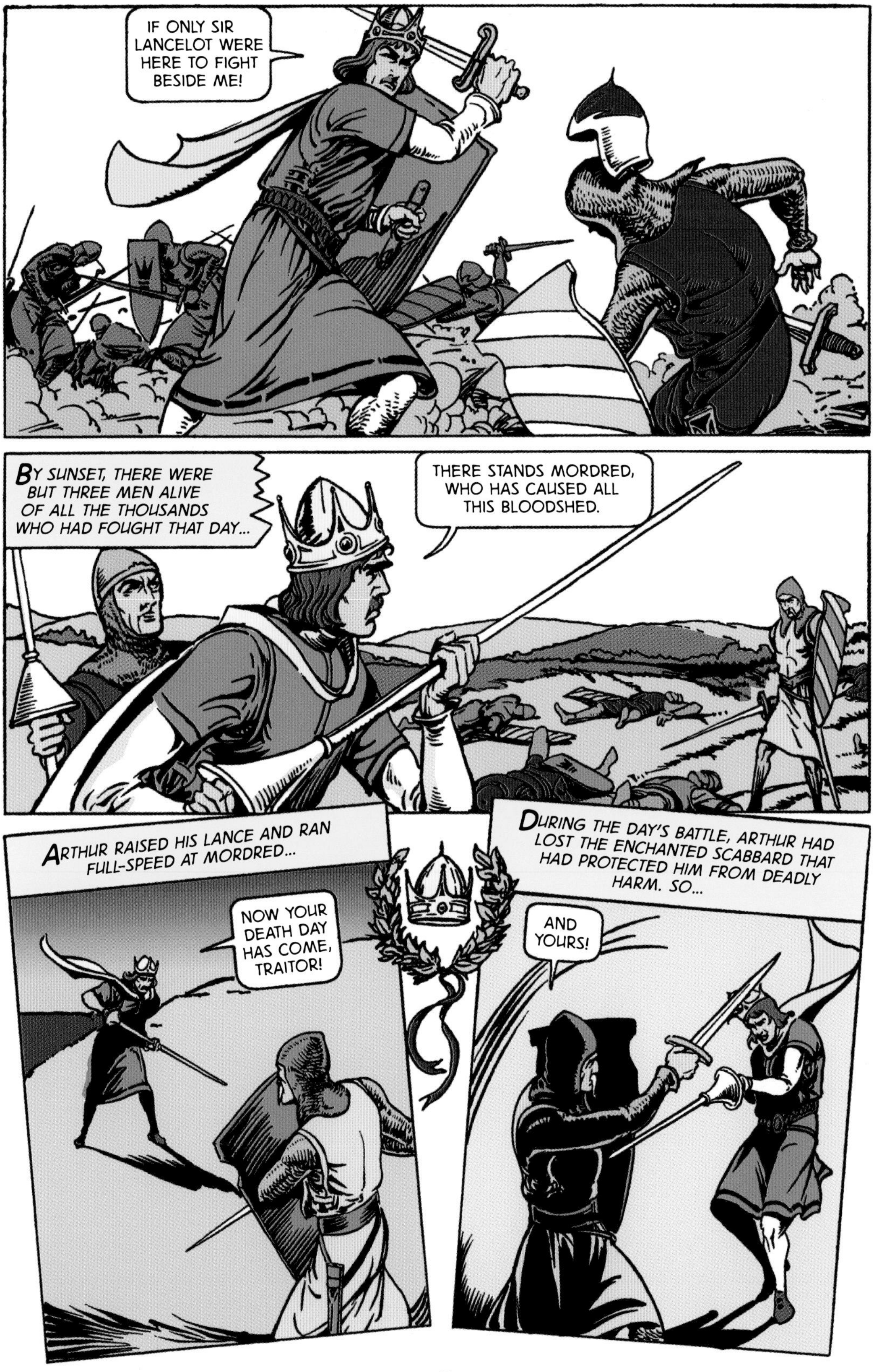
IF ONLY SIR LANCELOT WERE HERE TO FIGHT BESIDE ME!
BY SUNSET, THERE WERE BUT THREE MEN ALIVE OF ALL THE THOUSANDS WHO HAD FOUGHT THAT DAY...
THERE STANDS MORDRED, WHO HAS CAUSED ALL THIS BLOODSHED.
ARTHUR RAISED HIS LANCE AND RAN FULL-SPEED AT MORDRED...
NOW YOUR DEATH DAY HAS COME, TRAITOR!
DURING THE DAY'S BATTLE, ARTHUR HAD LOST THE ENCHANTED SCABBARD THAT HAD PROTECTED HIM FROM DEADLY HARM. SO...
AND YOURS!

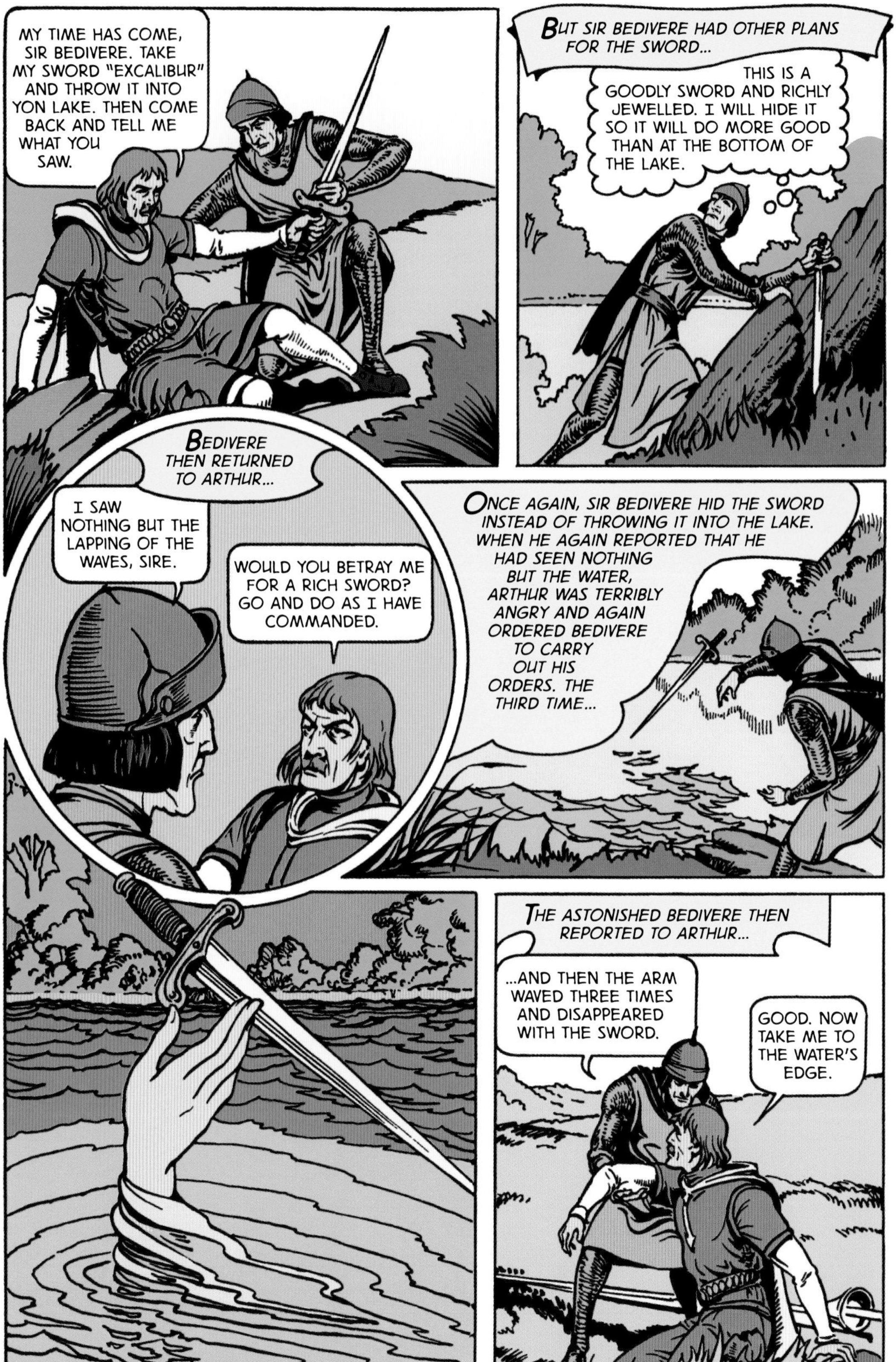
MY TIME HAS COME, SIR BEDIVERE. TAKE MY SWORD "EXCALIBUR" AND THROW IT INTO YON LAKE. THEN COME BACK AND TELL ME WHAT YOU SAW.
BUT SIR BEDIVERE HAD OTHER PLANS FOR THE SWORD...
THIS IS A GOODLY SWORD AND RICHLY JEWELLED. I WILL HIDE IT SO IT WILL DO MORE GOOD THAN AT THE BOTTOM OF THE LAKE.
BEDIVERE THEN RETURNED TO ARTHUR...
I SAW NOTHING BUT THE LAPPING OF THE WAVES, SIRE.
WOULD YOU BETRAY ME FOR A RICH SWORD? GO AND DO AS I HAVE COMMANDED.
ONCE AGAIN, SIR BEDIVERE HID THE SWORD INSTEAD OF THROWING IT INTO THE LAKE. WHEN HE AGAIN REPORTED THAT HE HAD SEEN NOTHING BUT THE WATER, ARTHUR WAS TERRIBLY ANGRY AND AGAIN ORDERED BEDIVERE TO CARRY OUT HIS ORDERS. THE THIRD TIME...
THE ASTONISHED BEDIVERE THEN REPORTED TO ARTHUR...
...AND THEN THE ARM WAVED THREE TIMES AND DISAPPEARED WITH THE SWORD.
GOOD. NOW TAKE ME TO THE WATER'S EDGE.

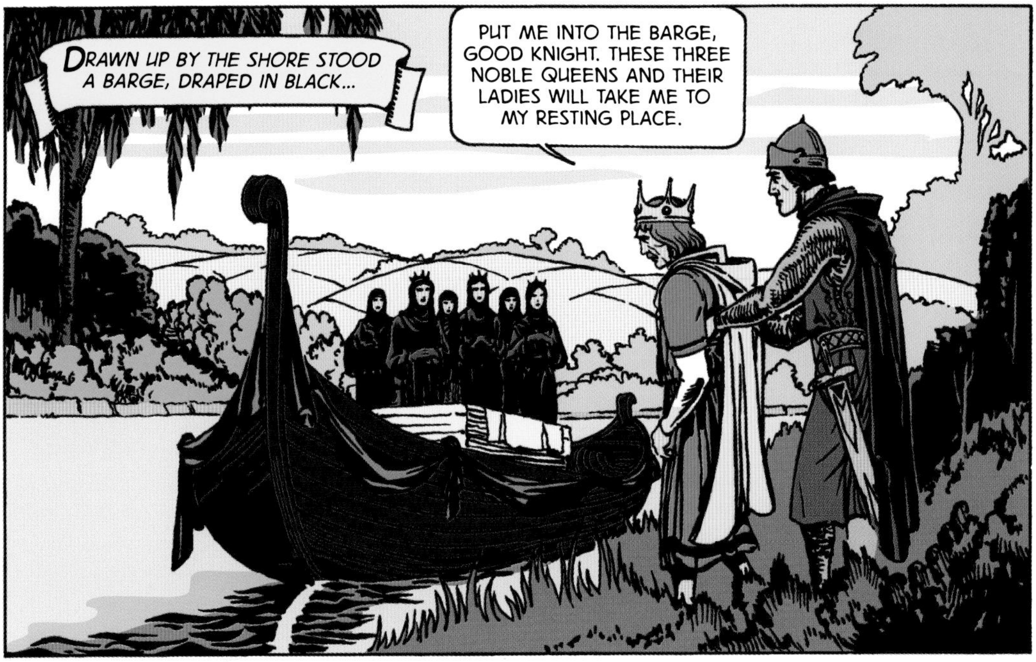
DRAWN UP BY THE SHORE STOOD A BARGE, DRAPED IN BLACK...
PUT ME INTO THE BARGE, GOOD KNIGHT. THESE THREE NOBLE QUEENS AND THEIR LADIES WILL TAKE ME TO MY RESTING PLACE.

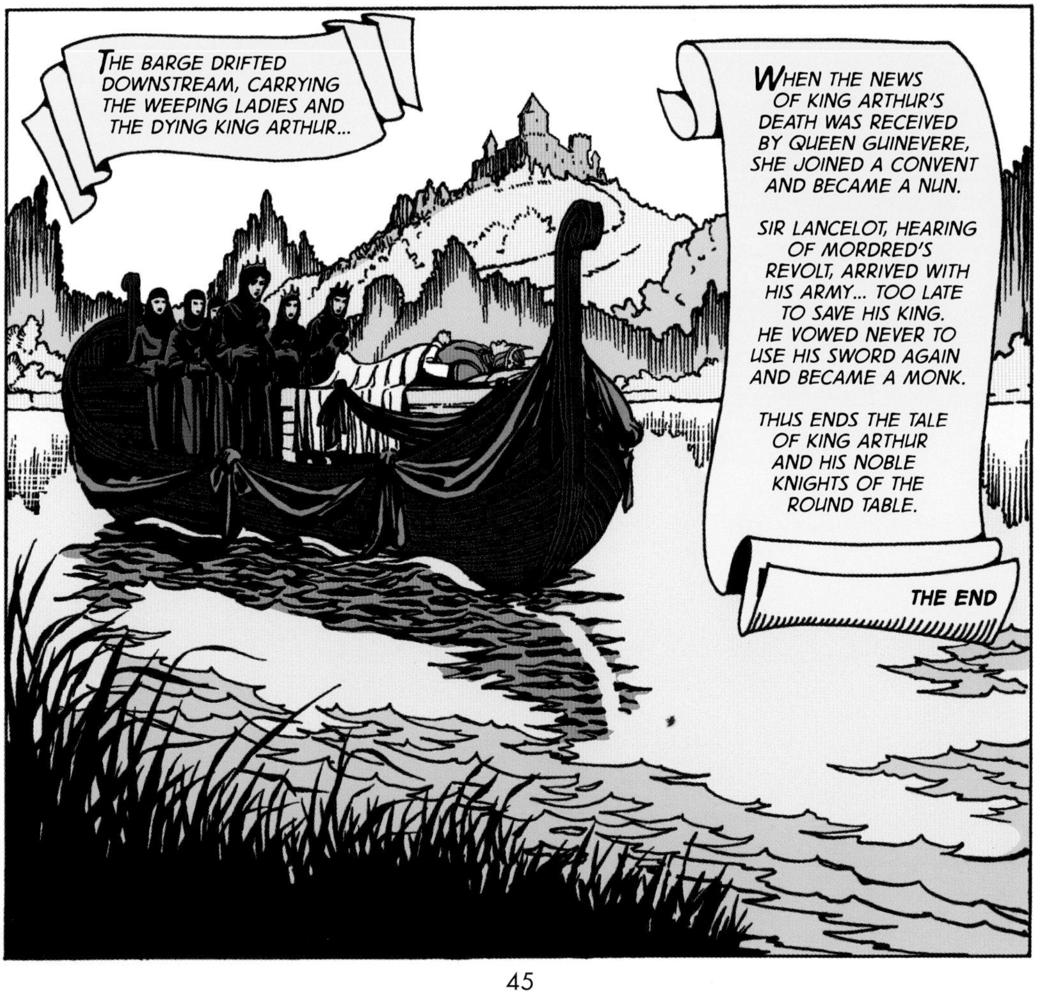
THE BARGE DRIFTED DOWNSTREAM, CARRYING THE WEEPING LADIES AND THE DYING KING ARTHUR...
WHEN THE NEWS OF KING ARTHUR'S DEATH WAS RECEIVED BY QUEEN GUINEVERE, SHE JOINED A CONVENT AND BECAME A NUN.
SIR LANCELOT, HEARING OF MORDRED'S REVOLT, ARRIVED WITH HIS ARMY... TOO LATE TO SAVE HIS KING. HE VOWED NEVER TO USE HIS SWORD AGAIN AND BECAME A MONK.
THUS ENDS THE TALE OF KING ARTHUR AND HIS NOBLE KNIGHTS OF THE ROUND TABLE.
THE END

Themes

The legend of King Arthur and his Knights of the Round Table is one of the most enduring tales in western history, and has existed for over 1000 years! Knights of the Round Table were those men awarded the highest order of Chivalry at the Court of King Arthur. The table at which they met was specially designed to have no head or foot, demonstrating the equality of all those seated around it.

Geoffrey of Monmouth is usually regarded as one of the first to bring the Arthurian legend to life, though there are scattered works, references and oral traditions from all ages. However a number of essential elements that make up the Arthurian world didn't appear in Geoffrey's tales. The heroes Lancelot and Percival were nowhere to be seen. There was no Camelot, no Holy Grail, and more importantly, no Round Table.

It wasn't until 1155, when the Anglo-Norman author from Jersey, Wace, wrote down his *Roman de Brut* (an elaboration of Geoffrey of Monmouth's *Historia Regum Britanniae*), that the Round Table was first introduced into the Arthurian legend.

Even in legend, Knights were usually of noble birth. They were a mixed bunch of minor kings and princes, dukes, counts (or earls), and barons. They formed the backbone of Arthur's army, with expensive armour and war-horses. Although in fact, armoured 'knights' weren't a reality for many, many years after the legends first began.

When knights attended a meeting or council at the King's main hall, those who sat at the head of the table, closer to the king, would usually have precedence over others. This meant that knights sitting lower down the table would be envious of those having a 'higher' ranking.

To resolve this problem, Arthur decided to have his council table constructed in a rounded shape. This unique design made all knights equal, whether he was a minor king or a high ranking baron. Now, no one knight would have precedence over others. Thus the famous Round Table actually began life as a political tool!

From this time onwards, the knights in Arthur's company became known as the "Knights of the Round Table". These knights were loyal, gallant, renowned for their strength and courage, for their skill in combat and warfare, their bravery and honour.

In *Le Morte D'Arthur* (1485), Sir Thomas Malory describes the Knights' code of chivalry as:

• To never do outrage nor murder
• Always to flee treason
• To by no means be cruel but to give mercy unto him who asks for mercy
• To always do ladies, gentlewomen and widows succour, upon pain of death
• Not to take up battles in wrongful quarrels for love or worldly goods

The knights vary from version to version and the number of knights varies from 12 to as many as 150, but here is one possible list:

Agravain • Bedivere • Bors
Calogrenant • Caradoc • Dagonet
Dinadan • Gaheris • Galahad
Gareth • Gawain • Geraint • Kay
Lamorak • Lancelot • Lionel
Palamedes • Percival • Safir
Sagramore • Tristan • Ywain

The Knights of the Round Table in Films

The story of The Knights of the Round Table has been the subject of several film adaptations, each with their own interpretation of the legend.

In 1953, Robert Taylor starred as Lancelot in MGM's *Knights of the Round Table*, with Mel Ferrer as Arthur and Ava Gardner as Guinevere. The film was the second in an unofficial trilogy coming between *Ivanhoe* (1952) and *The Adventures of Quentin Durward* (1955). As with later films, the love interest between Lancelot and Guinevere and their resistance to the attraction and the tensions generated by it provides a major part of the story, and is based on Book VII of Malory's *Le Morte d'Arthur*: "Sir Launcelot and Queen Gwenyvere".

In 1963, Disney gave the tale its own animated version from T. H. White's book *The Sword in the Stone*, with Merlin able to provide as wide an array of magical tricks as animation is able to create.

Camelot, released in 1967, gave us the film version of Lerner and Loewe's very successful musical - first staged on Broadway in 1960. The unlikely casting of Richard Harris as Arthur, Vanessa Redgrave as Guinevere and Franco Nero as Lancelot worked extremely well. The illicit love affair was very much to the fore.

The legend of the Knights of the Round Table was given the special brand of Monty Python humour in the 1975 film *Monty Python and the Holy Grail*. It was the troupe's first feature-length film of original material and it generally spoofs the legend of King Arthur's quest to find the Holy Grail. The Python crew were never big on romance in their works and Lancelot and Guinevere don't connect in this one. In 2005, Eric Idle brought the work to the stage in a musical adaptation called *Spamalot* which to date has won three Tony Awards. The show played its final Broadway performance on January 11th, 2009, after 35 previews and 1,574 performances.

Excalibur is a 1981 fantasy film which retells the legend of King Arthur. Directed by John Boorman, it boasts a high quality cast including Nicol Williamson as Merlin, Liam Neeson as Gawain, Patrick Stewart as King Leodegrance and Helen Mirren as Morgana Le Fay. Much of the film centres around the love affair of Lancelot and Guinevere. The film is primarily an adaptation of Malory's *Le Morte D'Arthur*.

Hollywood returned again to the legend in 1995 with *First Knight*, a Romantic fantasy adventure. It starred Richard Gere as Lancelot, Julia Ormond as Guinevere and Sean Connery as King Arthur. It was quite successful at the box office but not critically acclaimed. The film is noteworthy for its absence of Merlin and any magical elements at all.

Less than ten years later, in 2004, *King Arthur* was released, directed by Antoine Fuqua. It starred Clive Owen as the title character and Keira Knightley as Guinevere. The producers of the film claimed to present a historically accurate version of the Arthurian legends, supposedly inspired by new archaeological findings. The accuracy of these claims is subject to debate, but the film is unusual in representing Arthur as a Roman officer rather than a medieval Knight.

Arthur's Family Tree - According to Geoffrey of Monmouth

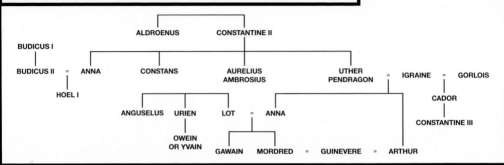

ALDROENUS
CONSTANTINE II
BUDICUS I
BUDICUS II = ANNA
CONSTANS
AURELIUS AMBROSIUS
UTHER PENDRAGON = IGRAINE = GORLOIS
HOEL I
ANGUSELUS
URIEN
LOT = ANNA
CADOR
CONSTANTINE III
OWEIN OR YVAIN
GAWAIN
MORDRED = GUINEVERE = ARTHUR

Arthur's Family Tree - According to Sir Thomas Malory

LEODEGRANCE
UTHER = IGRAINE = DUKE OF TINTAGEL
GUINEVERE = ARTHUR = MORGAWSE = LOT
ELAINE = NENTRES
MORGAN LE FAY = URIEN
MORDRED
GAWAIN
GAHERIS
AGRAVAIN
GARETH
GALESHIN
YVAIN
GUINGLAIN

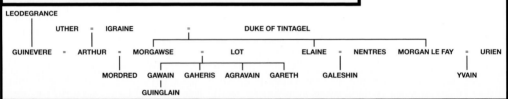

Excalibur

Excalibur is the legendary sword of King Arthur, often attributed with magical powers and associated with the rightful sovereignty of Great Britain. Sometimes Excalibur and the Sword in the Stone (the 'proof' of Arthur's lineage) are said to be the same weapon, but in most versions they are considered separate. The sword was associated with the Arthurian legend from the very first tales. In Welsh, the sword is called Caledfwlch.

In *Culhwch and Olwen*, it is one of Arthur's most valuable possessions and is used by Arthur's warrior Llenlleawg the Irishman to kill the Irish king Diwrnach while stealing his magical cauldron. Caledfwlch is thought to derive from the legendary Irish weapon Caladbolg, the lightning sword of Fergus mac Roich. Caladbolg was also known for its incredible powers and was carried by some of Ireland's greatest heroes.

Though not named as Caledfwlch, Arthur's sword is described vividly in *The Dream of Rhonabwy*, one of the tales associated with the *Mabinogion* thus:

> *"Then they heard Cadwr Earl of Cornwall being summoned, and saw him rise with Arthur's sword in his hand, with a design of two chimeras on the golden hilt; when the sword was unsheathed what was seen from the mouths of the two chimeras was like two flames of fire, so dreadful that it was not easy for anyone to look. At that, the host settled and the commotion subsided, and the earl returned to his tent."*
>
> - translated by Jeffrey Gantz

Geoffrey of Monmouth's *History of the Kings of Britain* (*Historia Regum Britanniae*) is the first non-Welsh source to speak of the sword. Geoffrey says the sword was forged in Avalon and changes the name "Caledfwlch" to Caliburn or Caliburnus.